FINALLY HOME IN WILLOW HEIGHTS

WILLOW HEIGHTS SERIES BOOK TWO

ABIGAIL BECK

CHAPTER 1

"*B*reakfast in bed!" Mary Elle announced as she walked into Melanie's room. Melanie didn't say a word. She simply turned on her side as tears slowly streamed down her face. Mary Elle placed the tray of food on the bedside table and sat next to her on the bed.

"Oh honey," she said as she ran her fingers through Melanie's straight black hair.

"Is something wrong with me?" Melanie asked as she cried.

It truly broke Mary Elle's heart to see her daughter this way. She wished there was a way to take the pain away. It had been a month since Melanie had shown up on her doorstep following her separation from her husband, Everett. Mary Elle worried she didn't see Melanie getting any better. Having gone through a divorce herself not long ago, she knew there wasn't exactly a time frame for the healing process.

"There is absolutely nothing wrong with you, honey."

"You're supposed to say that. You're my mother."

"I say it because it's the truth. Please sit up and eat this delicious breakfast I prepared just for you."

"I'm really not hungry," Melanie said, but sat up, anyway.

Mary Elle studied her daughter. She had always been fair skinned, but she was looking very pale and thin.

"Eat for the baby."

Melanie patted her growing bump and said, "All I've ever wanted was to be a mom."

"I know, honey. You will still be a mom. You will be an amazing mom. We may not know why things happen how they do, but I can assure you that God would never throw anything at you that you can't handle."

"I feel like such a fool."

"Why? You did nothing wrong."

"I knew Everett wasn't the one, mom. I knew it a long time ago. Shortly after we got married, I realized I had made a mistake, but I was too proud to admit it. I should've corrected my mistake."

Mary Elle had often wondered why Melanie stuck it through with Everett. She had noticed many times that they didn't seem happy with each other, but she didn't know why Melanie hadn't ended it before it got to this. Now she was understanding a little more.

She patted Melanie's knee and said, "It's ok to make mistakes. We learn from them, Mel. Maybe you wanted it to become true and thought time would make it work. It doesn't matter. You are carrying a baby inside of you now. A baby that you have wanted and loved all this time."

"Everett said he doesn't want the responsibility and pressure of a baby right now. He blames me for everything."

"Give him time. When he sees the baby, he'll love it too."

"No, mom. He's made up his mind. He said he only agreed to try and have a baby because he thought we wouldn't be able to conceive. I don't know that I want to have him in the baby's life if he's going to resent the baby."

"I know it may not seem like it right now, but things will work out. Everything will be okay."

"I'm scared. I never thought I would be a single mom. How will I raise a child without a dad? What will I tell it when it asks where its dad is?"

Mary Elle did what she did best. She hugged Melanie. She didn't have the right words to say, and she did not know what the future held, but she knew that the baby would have a wonderful life and would lack nothing, especially not love.

Melanie finally ate breakfast and got out of bed. She had moved in with Mary Elle, leaving everything behind in NYC. She had her essentials, and she said that's all she needed.

Everett called Mary Elle a few days after Melanie showed up to let her know he was shipping Melanie's furniture and items she had left behind when she came down to be with her. Mary Elle and her boyfriend, Thomas had taken the things to a storage unit in the next town over once they arrived.

She hadn't mentioned anything to Melanie to not upset her. The apartment she and Everett had lived in was under Everett's name, even though they both paid the mortgage. He would sell it and keeping all the money. Since they never had a prenup or any agreement, Melanie decided not to fight him on it. Mary Elle understood her. She wanted to move on and not have anything tying her to him for much longer.

Thomas visited often and brought Melanie flowers and goods from the bakery. He always asked Mary Elle if Melanie was having any cravings that he might be able to get her. Thomas' attentiveness and kindness touched Mary Elle. He had turned out to be so much more than she could've ever imagined. She hoped and prayed that Melanie would find someone to show her how great love could be.

Tiffany her youngest, had planned to visit them soon, but hadn't been able to because she had just started a new job. She had graduated from the University and had landed a great job at an up-and-coming new hotel in North Carolina.

Michael, Mary Elle's eldest, and only son, couldn't come visit Melanie but had called her several times to congratulate her on the pregnancy and to encourage her to keep her head up and to tell her jokes to make her laugh again. He mentioned he would visit for Thanksgiving and Mary Elle couldn't wait to have all her kids together again.

Mary Elle's sister, DeeAnn and best friend, Rita had also shown Melanie an immense amount of support. Rita tried getting Melanie to do some color therapy and keep her mind occupied.

Even Bill, Mary Elle's ex-husband and Melanie's father, had called Melanie several times and had also planned on visiting them soon but had a hectic schedule at work for the next couple of weeks.

It seemed as if this terrible situation was bringing everyone closer to each other in a strange way. Mary Elle was glad to see that she had the support of so many friends and family. Melanie also felt the same way and thanked everyone that was there helping her.

A few friends from NYC started sending Melanie gifts for the baby. They all knew how much Melanie wanted this baby and how much she had to go through to get here. Mary Elle gave Melanie one last glance and was happy to see that she was eating her breakfast. She hated leaving her alone, but she had to get to work. Today they would host a business retreat at Willow Acres, and she had been looking forward to this for months now.

* * *

MELANIE SLEPT like a baby that night. This was the first night where she hadn't stayed up all night thinking about Everett and how things had ended the way they had. She could finally sleep and dream again, which she hadn't done since she left New York.

The weeks following their separation had been a blur. She spent a lot of time wallowing in self-pity and beating herself up. Melanie was tired of thinking back on old memories and all the excuses she had made for him then. She had been such a fool.

No matter how bad things got, she always held on to hope. Every time things got really bad, she reminded herself of times when they had been good and that's what had kept her going. She hadn't been sure how Everett would respond to the baby news. She had been hesitant to tell him, but she never thought that he would react the way he did.

She blamed herself more than anything, and it plagued her with this feeling of shame that she couldn't shake. Her family had been nothing but understanding, which made things a little easier. However, she couldn't help feeling like a failure. Not only was her marriage over, but now she would also be a single mother. How had life ended up this way?

Melanie hated feeling this way. This wasn't who she was. She had never been a quitter and she couldn't let this situation ruin her life. Let alone over a guy. Melanie was going to have a baby, and she was going to show everyone, including Everett, that she was capable of this.

She sat up in the bed and decided that it was time she got her like back together; she started by taking a long relaxing bath before heading down to the kitchen to make breakfast for everyone.

"Good morning, sunshine." Mary Elle said as she reached the kitchen and noticed Melanie.

"Good morning mom, I wanted to surprise you." Melanie

said as she grabbed a cup from the cupboard and prepared a coffee for her mother.

"It smells wonderful. What are you making?"

"I'm making our favorites, pancakes, eggs, bacon and coffee."

"It smells delicious. I'm so happy to see you up so early. Do you have any plans?"

"No, but I had a great dream. I saw myself with the baby and we were happy and healthy. Which made me realize that's all that truly matters."

A light knock on the front door interrupted them, and Thomas appeared in the kitchen shortly after. Melanie still couldn't get over the fact that no one in Willow Heights ever locked their front door.

"It smells delicious in here!" Thomas said as he went over to Mary Elle and placed a kiss on her cheek.

Melanie noticed her mom blush and quickly glance her way nervously. She wasn't used to seeing her mom with a man that wasn't her father, but it made her happy to see the way Thomas treated her. He respected her mother and valued her opinions. He was always available for her and offered her the support she needed. She'd never seen her mother have such a fulfilling relationship with her father like this and it made her so proud to see her mom so happy and in love.

"Thank you for coming, Thomas." Melanie said as she gave him a side hug. Melanie texted Thomas that morning, inviting him over for breakfast. She wanted to show her appreciation to him for how welcoming he had been. Though she had been in a rough spot, she didn't overlook how attentive he'd been with her.

"I wouldn't have missed it." Thomas said as he took a seat next to Mary Elle.

"I hope I'm not late," DeeAnn said as she hurried into the

kitchen, still in her pajamas and her curly hair sticking up all over the place. She took a seat next to Melanie and quickly dug in to the food. "Oh, this is so good!"

Melanie smiled and said, "I'm glad you could make it. We've missed you the last few days."

"I was tying up some loose ends in Savannah, but I am happy to be settling in now," DeeAnn said as she poured herself some orange juice.

Melanie was pleased to hear that; DeeAnn and Mary Elle had a falling out at a young age and because of that they had lost touch. DeeAnn staying in Willow Heights gave them an opportunity to make up for lost time and make fresh memories.

"Are you nervous about starting at a new school?" Thomas asked her.

"Sure am. I am both excited and nervous about it. I met a lot of the parents and kids over the summer, but I haven't met the principal yet."

School had already started and DeeAnn was starting her new teaching job at Willow Heights Middle School. She told them she was nervous about her first day at work; she had made friends, but the school was a couple miles out into town.

Mrs. Adelman had gotten her the job without an interview, just based on recommendations, and this added pressure to her. So far, everyone had been extremely nice over the phone when they contacted DeeAnn about the job. Things here were done a little differently here than in Savannah. DeeAnn met a lot of parents and students that had taken part in the summer camp, and she knew most of them attended Willow Heights Middle School.

"Don't be nervous Aunt D, I'm positive all the kids and parents will love you."

"Thanks Melanie. Also, you look so beautiful with your little baby bump."

"Thank you. Before we know it, this baby will be one of your students!" Melanie said with a laugh while rubbing her belly.

Thomas cleared his throat and nervously said, "Melanie, this might not be the best time to bring this up, but I've been meaning to talk to you."

"What is it?" Melanie said, growing concerned. Thomas wasn't usually the nervous type.

"As you know, we are trying to bring in more business to Willow Acres. We have been doing great with all the amazing events your mother has been wonderfully planning," he said as he glanced at Mary Elle and Melanie couldn't help but notice the pink tint that had crept in her mother's cheeks.

"David and I have been talking about revamping the website and also getting an in-house photographer to offer our clients for the events. We would love for you to join our team."

"I would love to!"

"Are you sure? It's not a fancy New York job, but we would love to have you. Please don't feel pressured to take it if you're not ready," Thomas said.

"Thomas, I would love to nothing more than to join your team. I have no plans to return to New York. Willow Heights feels like just the place for my new beginning. You all don't know this, but I quit my job in NYC and I've been worried about money since the baby is due in a few months. I have some savings but I am quickly learning that babies are expensive."

"Great. You can come in on Monday with me if you're up for it," Mary Elle said, beaming.

"Yes, I think that is a wonderful way to move forward." DeeAnn chipped in.

Breakfast was a delight. Melanie was feeling better. She had felt the baby move inside her, and that made everything feel much more real. Since moving to Willow Heights, Melanie had found a good OBGYN in the next town over that would be her new doctor. She was already taking her prenatal vitamins and was now embracing her baby. Before, she felt horrible because she was keeping the baby a secret from Everett. Then when she finally told him he went off on her and blamed her for trying to sabotage his career. That was when she had enough, and left Everett to keep her baby safe and away from a toxic environment.

Her key priority was the baby and keeping the baby happy and healthy. She had books on pregnancy and was learning how the baby can also feel what the mother is feeling and did not want the baby to feel any sadness like she was. She decided to be strong and carry on.

* * *

MARY ELLE SAT on her back porch swing next to Thomas after that wonderful breakfast Melanie had prepared for them. Mary Elle had mentioned recently that she always wanted a wooden swing back here. A week later, Thomas surprised her with a swing that he made himself. Her heart warmed at the memory.

She glanced over at Thomas and was surprised to see that he was watching her.

"Penny for your thoughts?" She said to him.

"Just wondering how I got so lucky," Thomas said with that smile of his that made Mary Elle's heart skip a few beats.

"Thomas, you little sweet talker," Mary Elle said as she snuggled in closer to him.

"It's not sweet talking if it's the truth."

Mary Elle let out a sigh.

"Hey, what's wrong?" Thomas asked, pulling away to get a closer look at her.

"I'm just worried about Melanie. She's never had the best luck in relationships and I'm afraid that she'll close herself off from anyone new now."

"She's not even divorced yet and you're worried she won't find someone new?" Thomas asked gently. Mary Elle realized how silly it sounded once she heard it coming out of his mouth.

"I'm her mom. I'm supposed to worry about these things," she said with a shrug. No matter how old her kids got, she could never stop worrying about them. She was starting to see that no matter how grown they were, a mother's job was never done.

"Melanie will be alright." Thomas said confidently and sat back, putting his arm around Mary Elle.

Mary Elle wished she could be as sure as he sounded, but she wasn't so sure. She felt sick to her stomach with worry over Melanie's future. She'd heard of many women suffering from postpartum depression after pregnancy and she feared that would be the case here.

"I hope you're right," she said softly.

"What if this is what's best for her?"

"What do you mean?"

"Divorce isn't the worst outcome sometimes. Look at us," he said, motioning between them.

"You have a point," Mary Elle said as she remembered how lonely and sad Melanie had always seemed during her marriage. "I just want her to be happy."

"What if, instead of thinking what can go wrong, you imagine what could go right?"

"See? This is why I keep you around," Mary Elle said with a smile. Thomas was right. Melanie was going to be alright and she would make sure of it.

"There actually is something else on my mind that I hadn't mentioned, because of everything you have going on," Thomas said.

"Oh? What is it?"

"Patty mentioned she saw Wyatt pocketing some money from the restaurant last week."

"What are you going to do?"

"I heard his mother lost her job recently, but I've been so busy that I hadn't asked if they needed help. I feel terrible. Wyatt is a great kid and I know he would never do something like this if he wasn't desperate."

"You're right. I would never expect that from him. He is such a good kid. Honestly, I would never expect that from anyone at Willow Acres, we have a great team."

Thomas nodded, but Mary Elle could tell his thoughts were somewhere else. She made a mental note to try and find a way to help Wyatt. Thomas filled Mary Elle in on the young boy's history. His mother had raised him alone after his father left them a little after Wyatt was born. His father had a history of abusing alcohol, and it had been rumored that he also physically abused Wyatt's mother.

Mary Elle couldn't fathom how difficult this must have been for Wyatt. She felt for the boy and made it a mission to find a way to help him. She may not have known him for very long, but she knew how hardworking he was and that this was completely out of character for him.

CHAPTER 2

On Monday morning, Melanie wasn't sure if it was morning sickness or nerves making her stomach feel uneasy. She had met most of the Willow Acres staff before, but she didn't want them to think she had only gotten the job because of her mother's relationship to Thomas.

She was a talented photographer and nothing brought her more joy than seeing her clients' faces when she showed them the images from their photoshoots. There really was no way to put a price on capturing moments they could treasure for the rest of their lives.

"I have my doctor's appointment in a few days. Would you be able to come with me?" Melanie asked Mary Elle in hopes that distracting herself by talking about the baby would calm her nerves.

"Of course!" Mary Elle said without a second thought.

Melanie knew her mother loved babies and had already started planning the baby shower, the baby room, baby names, everything, and anything you could think of baby related. She was glad that she could share this experience with her.

While living in New York, she had often worried about becoming a mother and not having any family close by. Mary Elle and Tiffany were her best friends and she couldn't imagine them not being around to see her kids grow up.

"Are you ready to head to work?" Melanie asked.

"Let me grab my purse and we can go."

"Ok, I'll wait for you in the car." Melanie said as she petted Mittens on her way to the car. Mittens purred; she loved the attention.

DURING THEIR DRIVE TO WORK, Melanie asked Mary Elle if she'd heard from Everett. Mary Elle told her he called a while ago to say he would mail some of her things. That response unsettled Melanie, but she let it go. There wasn't much she could do, except move forward.

As they drove up to Willow Acres, the foliage was changing. You could feel autumn was on its way.

All the Willow Acres staff were outside when they arrived. Melanie knew Mary Elle told them she was coming, and they wanted to welcome her and make her feel right at home. One thing Melanie had noticed about Willow Acres since her first visit was that the people were genuinely nice and caring. They didn't see each other as co-workers, but more like family.

"Welcome Melanie," the group said cheerfully.

"Thank you," Melanie said, a little shy. She did not want to make a big deal out of it, but she knew her mom would not let that happen.

Thomas came over to welcome Melanie and introduce her as the onsite photographer and webmaster. He also showed her the office space they setup for her. She would be right next door to her mother. Melanie loved the bay window with a bench to look out into the forest. She envisioned herself sitting here with her baby and a sense of peace came over her.

"Do you like it?" Thomas asked

"I love it. Thank you, Thomas. I wasn't expecting so much on my first day," she said as she pulled Thomas into a hug, which surprised both of them. She had never been the hugging kind. That was her mom's thing.

"We are just happy to have such a talented photographer amongst us," Thomas said with a big smile on his face.

"You're too kind. Thank you for everything."

"Well, let me know if you need anything or if you're craving anything. Dean can cook up anything in no time for you," Thomas said as he made his way out and left Melanie alone to finish setting up.

Melanie had brought a few items of her own to make her office feel like her own. She placed a small bonsai tree on her desk, her favorite peony candle, and other small Knick knacks.

Once she was done, she stepped back to look at the finished product. She let out a small gasp when she glanced out the office window and saw a mama deer with her two small fawns. For some reason, that made her get teary-eyed and she absent-mindedly placed a hand on her small baby bump.

* * *

"A lot on your mind?" Thomas asked as he leaned in the doorway to Mary Elle's office.

Mary Elle jumped in her seat and placed her hand over her heart, "Thomas! I didn't see you there. Come in," she said, waving him in.

"I didn't mean to startle you. Is everything okay? Is there

anything you need?" He asked as he took the seat in front of her desk.

"Everything is fine. I am just worried about Melanie as per usual, but I think being here will help her."

"If Melanie is anything like her mother, I am sure she'll be okay in no time," Thomas said with a wink.

"I hope you're right, but as a mother you never stop worrying."

Thomas came around behind Mary Elle and placed his hands on her shoulder before kissing the top of her head and saying, "Give her time. Divorce isn't easy on any of us. She's also going to be a single mother now, which she wasn't counting on."

Mary Elle knew Thomas was right. She had gone through something similar not long ago, and she understood completely that only time could heal Melanie's heart.

"Hey love birds," David said as he came into Mary Elle's office.

"You're back early." Thomas said as he hugged David and clapped him on the back. David had been gone for a week to celebrate his friend's bachelor's party. They had taken a hiking trip to Grand Teton National Park.

"How was Wyoming?"

"It was amazing! We did so many hikes. The views were breathtaking. Here. let me show you a video."

They huddled close together and watched a couple of videos David had taken while on his hike with a small action camera he had strapped to his chest.

"Oh no, I can't look!" Mary Elle said, covering her eyes.

David laughed. "It wasn't that bad. You just had to watch your step and keep your balance."

"I'm glad to have you back with us in one piece," Mary Elle said

"Melanie started today; she should be in her office.

Maybe you can go over some projects with her," Thomas said.

"How is she doing?" David asked.

"She's hanging in there." Thomas told him as they walked over to Melanie's office together.

* * *

"HEY MELANIE, WELCOME TO WILLOW ACRES," David said as he made his way into Melanie's office.

"Hi stranger. Welcome Back!"

"Let's talk about projects,"

"Wow, so you're jumping into business mode that quickly?"

"No better way to rip the band aid off," he said with a shrug.

"I heard you went on a trip. How was it?"

"It was amazing. We had a great time out there. We did a lot of hikes. Here, look at these," he said as he handed Melanie his phone.

"These photos are amazing; you have an eye for sunsets. What camera did you use?"

"Oh, just a small action camera."

"It looks like you had an amazing time with the guys."

"It was a friend's bachelor's party trip. Matthew wanted something different and none of us had been to Wyoming before."

"The Tetons have always been on my bucket list. With the baby on the way, it might be awhile before I do any hiking again. Anyway, you wanted to talk business. well I have some ideas for revamping the website." Melanie said as she brought out her notepad.

She read out all her ideas to David, and he mostly sat back

nodding and would jump in whenever he thought of something to add.

"I have a confession to make," David said once they were done going through Melanie's list.

"What is it?"

"When Thomas mentioned you coming on board, I wasn't so sure you would be the best fit for the job," He said, holding his hands up. "Let me finish... I saw the work you did for the magazine in New York and it was great, but I wasn't sure how you would do for a small-town farm. Watching you now and hearing your ideas, I've changed my mind."

"What made you change your mind?"

"Your passion. Photography is your passion, and it shows. You did amazing in New York because you have a great eye, but you're also full of ideas. Now you're here and look at your list; for someone that has never lived in a small-town, you understood the assignment."

"Thank you. I loved working in New York and putting my creativity to good use, but I really am looking forward to joining this team and capturing great memories for years to come."

David nodded and said, "I reviewed the photos you took last time. How do you feel about shooting new photos now that it's fall? We can have a new gallery with better photos of the entire area."

"That would work. I don't mind taking new photos and editing them."

"Great, let's get started,"

David and Melanie walked around Willow Acres and decided on the areas that needed new photos and some up keeping before the photoshoot. They also wanted to get Brittney to visit again and have her write another review of the venue. Mrs. Adelman also mentioned that she would like for Brittney to stay at her inn and write a review.

Working with David and the team at Willow Acres differed from working in NYC, where everything was fast-paced and hectic. People seemed less moody here, and she could take time to enjoy her surroundings.

* * *

MARY ELLE ARRIVED at the restaurant a few minutes earlier hoping to get a few minutes alone with Wyatt before Melanie joined her. The restaurant was busier than usual and Wyatt was rushing around, so she hadn't gotten to talk to him.

Melanie arrived and took her seat across from her mother and gave Wyatt her order.

"How's your first day going, sweetie?" Mary Elle asked Melanie as Wyatt headed to the kitchen for their drinks.

"Great. Everyone's been super nice, and this place has some type of magic because I've been so relaxed all day."

"It really is something else," Mary Elle said.

She watched as Melanie looked around and took all the natural beauty in that she rarely got to appreciate in the big city.

"This might sound crazy, but it's so different to hear the birds chirping and the small waves in the lake and not the blaring horns of cars in traffic or the subway train on the tracks. There is a wonderful calmness in this place."

"I know exactly what you mean," Mary Elle said, and she felt some of the worry that had been eating her up wash away.

"I also haven't thought about Everett all day, which is a first."

"That's fantastic Melanie. I know it's difficult to move on and I'm sure you have a lot of conflicting emotions you're dealing with, but honey, you're doing great."

"Thanks mom. How's your day, mom? Why aren't you having lunch with Thomas?"

"Oh, he's got a meeting with some construction people. He wants to expand and remodel the Inn here."

"That's nice. This place already has so much going on but it would be great to have the Inn operating again."

"Yes, after Brittney's first visit, we got a lot of interest in staying at the Inn, but Thomas had been too busy with everything else. Mrs. Adelman's Inn benefitted a lot from Brittney's review too."

"I heard. Mrs. Adelman let me know she had done some remodeling and wanted Brittney to stay at her Inn next time to write a review."

"That would be great. Who knew social media marketing would work so well?" Mary Elle said with a giggle.

Melanie had known the power of social media marketing and had been the one to suggest inviting her friend Brittney from New York. They had all been surprised at just how successful the campaign had been.

Mary Elle figured it had to do with everything going on in the world. Everyone just wanted to get away from the hustle and bustle and Willow Heights was just the place for that.

* * *

MARY ELLE SNUCK into the back kitchen once they finished their lunch. She was hoping to get some alone time with Wyatt. She hadn't brought it up to Melanie that she had an ulterior motive for having lunch at the restaurant today. Mary Elle usually packed a lunch for herself, but she really wanted to speak to Wyatt.

"Hey Wyatt, how's everything?" Mary Elle asked as she found him stocking the pantry.

Wyatt jumped at the sound of her voice, "Mary Elle, sorry I didn't hear you come in."

"Oh, sorry. I didn't mean to sneak up on you. How is everything?"

"Everything is okay," Wyatt said, as his eyes darted around the room.

Mary Elle could tell he was feeling uneasy.

"Everything alright at home?" Mary Elle asked, hoping that she wasn't being too pushy.

"Everything is fine. Thanks for asking." Wyatt said, clearing his throat and straightening his back.

"Well, I just wanted to say that Thomas and I were talking about you yesterday and we both agree that you are one of our top employees here. We love having you and if there's ever anything that you need... please don't hesitate to come find us."

Wyatt stood still and nodded, "Thank you, Mary Elle."

Mary Elle smiled and gave Wyatt's shoulder a small squeeze before heading out again. She figured he wasn't ready to talk yet. That would not stop her from sorting this out. She knew Thomas was right and that Wyatt wouldn't have done this unless he was absolutely desperate. She decided right then and there to pay Wyatt's mother a visit.

* * *

WHEN SHE ARRIVED at Wyatt's home, she noticed there were a couple of cars in the driveway. She didn't want to intrude and was about to head back to Willow Acres when she noticed that Wyatt's mother was outside and heading towards her car.

"May I help you?" She asked as she approached Mary Elle's car.

Mary Elle turned off her car and lowered the window, "Hi, I'm Mary Elle. I'm Wyatt's -"

"Yes, I know who you are." His mother said, not letting Mary Elle finish her sentence as she glanced back to her house uneasily. "Wyatt's not here. He's at work."

"I know, I actually came to look for you."

"Why?"

"I just wanted to talk. I know you lost your job recently, and I wanted to know if we could do anything to help. I know it must not be easy and,"

Mary Elle jumped, surprised when she heard a man's voice yell out, "Hey! What's taking so long?" she glanced back at the house and saw him standing in the doorway. She wasn't sure who he was. She knew Wyatt's dad wasn't around, and she had never seen this man before.

"Nothing, she was just leaving!" Wyatt's mother yelled back before turning back to Mary Elle and saying, "I appreciate you coming to check in, but we're good," and walked back to the house shutting the door behind her.

Mary Elle sat in her car, confused. What just happened? Who was that man? And why did Wyatt's mom seem so suspicious? There was definitely more going on than they had imagined.

CHAPTER 3

*M*elanie was lost in a trance taking pictures by the lake when she got a call from her soon to be ex-mother-in-law. She ignored the call. She wasn't ready to speak with anyone in Everett's family and if it was an emergency, she would leave a message, Melanie said to herself. There was no voicemail message left.

Melanie was instantly flooded with memories of her time with Everett and his family. She tried to not let any negative thoughts of what transpired with Everett bring her down. She had worked hard to crawl out of that black hole she had been in.

She remembered Rita telling her that taking deep breaths would help to clear her mind and re-focus on what was real and not the past or future. So, she sat down under a tree and closed her eyes and just took breaths and let things go. Melanie regained her strength again and realized that she had to be present in the moment as she felt her baby move around inside of her.

She whispered, "I know you're here with me too and you're helping me be strong."

* * *

THE FIRST FEW days flew by and on Wednesday night, Melanie found herself home alone. Mary Elle and Thomas had gone out on a date and DeeAnn had gone out with her new teacher friends. Tiffany called Melanie, and they chatted for a while. Melanie told her about her first day at work, and Tiffany told her about how things were going at her job. Tiffany asked about David, which Melanie suspected meant that Tiffany was interested in him, though she would never admit it.

"He's doing well. He just got back from his friend's bachelor trip. They went hiking."

"That's adventurous," Tiffany said.

"Yup, maybe you should come visit us soon."

"I just started this new job and Mrs. White, the general manager, isn't very fond of me." Tiffany said with a slightly worried tone.

"Oh, sorry, I've been so absorbed with my drama I hadn't realized you started a new job and had a terrible boss." Melanie said apologetically.

"It's okay. don't be so hard on yourself, Mel."

"Why did she hire you if she didn't like you?"

"It's complicated. Short story is, the staffing agency hired me."

"Oh, I see. I'm sure you'll win her over. You're a hard worker and incredibly smart."

"I hope so. She's been complaining about me, but I'm trying my best. It's just my best isn't good enough for her."

"I'm so sorry you're in that situation. I know how long you've dreamt of working in the industry."

"Yeah, but I don't have enough saved up to buy a charming little cottage or house to make it into a bed-and-breakfast yet and I don't want to ask mom and dad for money."

"I hear you. I'm so proud of you, Tiff. You've always been so smart and known what you've wanted. You've never settled, unlike me."

Melanie often wished she were more like Tiffany. She always knew what she wanted and never lost sight of her goals. Melanie had been so Starstruck when she met Everett that she made so many excuses for his behavior. She knew Tiffany would've never done that.

"I'm really sorry about what happened between you and Everett. Not surprised it happened, but he could've handled it better."

"What do you mean, not surprised?"

"Well, you both haven't been happy for a long time and it was obvious. I never saw a connection between you two. He handled this all wrong, but truthfully? He did you a favor. If he hadn't, you probably would've stayed with him for many more years."

"Why didn't you say anything before?"

"You wouldn't have listened, Mel."

"Maybe you're right, but I would appreciate you commenting next time you see me going down the wrong path."

"You won't. But if you do, I'll be there and I'll speak up. I love you, Mel."

"I love you too, my little big sister," Melanie said, using the nickname she and Michael had given Tiffany. Though she was the youngest of the three, she had always been the most level-headed.

"I have to go. I have to be at work at 5 AM tomorrow."

"Okay, have a good night."

"You too."

Melanie sat back, thinking back on her conversation with

Tiffany. How was it that everyone had seen how unhappy she'd been except for her?

Melanie got a few calls from friends back in NYC, but she didn't want to ruin her evening. Those calls went unanswered. It was too early to go to sleep, so she went to the grocery store to pick up a few things.

"Hey Melanie," said a familiar voice from behind. Melanie turned to find David and Cade.

"Hey guys, didn't expect to see you here."

"We're actually getting some essentials for the Willow Acres BBQ. You're coming right?" David asked

"Of course. I wouldn't miss it."

This weekend they were hosting the Willow Acres Family BBQ. Thomas made it a habit to get the staff together at least once every few months. Willow Acres usually closed on Sundays to the public, so it was the perfect time to get everyone together and for them to bring in their families and friends.

"Cade, I saw videos and photos of the trip you guys went on. It seemed very fun." Melanie said.

"It was the trip of a lifetime," he said.

"My favorite hikes are in the desert."

"Have you been out West?" Cade asked.

"Yes, I have been to the Grand Canyon. It's the most peaceful and beautiful place I've seen. Depending on the hour of the day, you capture different hues in the mountains."

"You've done photoshoots there?"

"Yes, and family trips as well. When I started off in photography, I was an elopement photographer."

"That's amazing. We need to get out more," David chimed in, patting Cade on his shoulder.

"We are having a little get together for by the lake next

weekend. You're welcome to join us. It'll be fun. We'll have BBQ and games." David said.

"Yea, sounds fun. My sister and Brittney might visit that weekend, though," Melanie replied.

"Invite them. The more the merrier."

Melanie finished her grocery shopping and headed home. She thought this would be a great way for Tiffany and David to get to know each other. She couldn't wait to tell her.

* * *

DeeAnn was in the kitchen when Melanie arrived and had some Chinese food for dinner.

"Hey Mel, I got your favorite," DeeAnn said, waving the takeout bag around.

"Thanks Aunt D, you're my favorite aunt."

"I'm your only aunt, silly!" DeeAnn said with a giggle.

"How was your first day at the new school?"

"It was good. Much slower paced than in Savannah. Which is funny because I used to always say Savannah was slow paced, which compared to Atlanta it is."

"I've noticed that everything here works at a much slower pace, but I like it."

DeeAnn nodded and asked, "How has your first week been going?"

"It's great. Everyone is so welcoming."

"How is my little niece or nephew doing?" DeeAnn asked in a baby voice as she bent down to Melanie's bump.

"This little baby is doing great, but making mommy extra tired and hungry all the time."

"Well, in that case, let's eats," DeeAnn said as she placed a plate of Chinese food in front of Melanie.

They ate and talked more about their first week at their new jobs. Melanie was feeling like her true self again. She had felt depressed for some time now, but that was fading away.

She was making new friends and was starting a new job where the environment wasn't toxic. She wasn't constantly arguing or begging for attention from anyone. Melanie felt a sense of freedom, although the loneliness tried to creep in at night. She knew this was only temporary, and in time, things would get better.

Rita, her mom's best friend, had gifted Melanie a Peaceful Lily plant and always reminded her to let things go, to have some alone time and release all negativity. At the beginning, it was difficult for Melanie because the pain was still very raw.

Her emotions were constantly fluctuating because of the hormonal change since she was pregnant. But knowing she was carrying and making a new human always gave her the strength to keep going and turned her frown upside down. It was all worth it.

* * *

Mary Elle sat in her office when her phone buzzed with a text message from Melanie.

"Mom, don't forget today we have the doctor's appointment at 2 p.m.," it said.

"I won't forget. We can leave together from work." Mary Elle quickly texted back and inserted a heart and baby emoji. She knew Melanie would be so proud of her enhanced texting skills.

"Hey honey, I'm going to run out for a bit, but I'll try to be back before you head out with Melanie," Thomas said as he popped his head into Mary Elle's office.

"What's going on?" Mary Elle asked, not liking the worried look on Thomas' face.

Thomas sighed and stepped into Mary Elle's office.

"What's going on?" Mary Elle asked again as she made her way over to him.

"Wyatt hasn't shown up to work the last two days. He hasn't answered Dean's calls or texts and he never called the main office to let us know he wasn't coming in."

"Is he okay?"

"I don't know, but I'm going to go find out."

Mary Elle cleared her throat and said, "Thomas, I need to tell you something."

"What is it? What's wrong?" Thomas asked as he raised her chin so she could meet his eyes.

His eyes were gentle and full of love and concern. Mary Elle knew it was time to come clean, "I tried talking to Wyatt a few days ago, and he seemed very jumpy and not like himself, so I went to his house to talk to his mom to see if there was anything we could do to help. I didn't get to talk to his mom much because some man interrupted us. I don't know who he is, but I didn't get a good feeling about him."

"Why didn't you tell me before? I would've gone with you."

"I know, and I'm sorry. I should've said something, but I didn't want you to get upset at me."

"I could never be upset with you," Thomas said, pulling her into a hug and kissing the top of her head, "I'm going with David and we will sort this out."

"Please be careful," Mary Elle said as she held him a little closer.

"I'll be back before you know it," Thomas said as he gave her another kiss.

As soon as Thomas left her office, Mary Elle went on her desktop computer. She went online and looked up Wyatt's social media and tried looking for his mother's page. Mary

Elle had to know who that man was and why Wyatt had suddenly started acting so out of character.

She said a brief prayer for Thomas and David to return safely and for everything to be okay with Wyatt and his family. She became so engrossed in her search for information that she was completely surprised when Melanie appeared in her office.

"Let's go, mom" Melanie said as she walked into Mary Elle's office.

"I'm ready. Are you excited?" Mary Elle asked. She decided not to tell Melanie about Wyatt or that Thomas and David had left a few hours ago and she hadn't heard from either of them since.

"Very. This is my first visit to this new doctor. I did a lot of research and I hope she's as good as everyone says she is," Melanie answered. Willow Heights was a tiny town with only one family doctor. Melanie had opted to go to Winding Creek, the next town over, which was bigger and had an OBGYN with excellent reviews.

"A lot of clients have talked about Dr. Banks and they all love her." Mary Elle shared.

"That's good. I need to find a Lamaze class in town or not too far away from here."

"I ordered you some books. I know you're not too much into reading, but these are good books. Also, Rita is sending you a meditation and Pilates DVD and book combo. She said it's important to stretch and meditate."

"I'm not sure if I'm flexible enough for Pilates right now, but it doesn't hurt to try."

Melanie felt extremely blessed to have so many people that wished her well and wanted her and the baby to be healthy and happy. She didn't expect things to start falling into place like this, but she loved every bit of it.

* * *

ON THEIR WAY to the doctor's office, Bill called. Not very long ago, she would have ignored his call after what he did to her mother, but since her separation from Everett, her father had been in constant contact with her. He often checked on her via text or quick emails to see how she was doing.

She understood now that relationships were complex, and sometimes; they fell apart at no fault to anyone. Both her parents were happier now than they had been when they were together, so it helped no one for her to hold a grudge against her father.

"Hi Dad, how are you?"

"I'm great honey. How are you feeling?"

"Good. Mom and I are on our way to the doctor. It's my first appointment with Dr. Banks. Also, I wanted to thank you for the gift basket you sent me, it was lovely."

"You're welcome. Sorry I haven't been able to visit you yet. I'm working on it."

"Don't worry Dad. Visit whenever you have time."

"I'll let you go now, but please let me know if you need anything. Say hello to your mother for me."

"I will, love you Dad"

"Me too, Melanie."

"Dad says hi," Melanie told Mary Elle as she hung up the call.

"How is he?"

"He says he's good and will visit soon."

"It would be nice for you to spend some time with him."

"Yeah, I just don't know about being around Barbara."

Barbara was Bill's new girlfriend and the reason Mary Elle and Bill divorced. She was a home-wrecker and Mary Elle's rival since high school. Mary Elle never imagined she would steal Bill away from her.

"Whatever you're comfortable with, sweetie," Mary Elle said, and Melanie knew she meant it. Even now, her mother still put her kids' needs first.

* * *

THEY ARRIVED at the doctor's office, and Melanie's nerves were all over the place. She got a little sad once she noticed all the happy couples in the waiting room. This is what it should have been like, she thought. She didn't regret things ending with Everett, but she wished she had a partner to experience this season of her life with.

Since she was a little girl, she had always wanted to be a mother and to have a family and now that she could finally experience it; it was nothing like she had imagined. Sensing what she was feeling, she felt her mom give her hand a small squeeze.

"Melanie Ford?" The nurse called out from the front desk area.

Melanie winced when she heard the nurse call her name. It had been a while since anyone had used her married name.

"That's me," she said as she quickly stood and made her way over with Mary Elle close behind.

Once in the exam room, the nurse introduced herself and took Melanie's vitals before leaving them to wait for Dr. Banks.

"How are you feeling?" Mary Elle asked.

"This is harder than I imagined," she responded with a sigh.

Mary Elle nodded with a sad smile. "This feeling is only temporary. Once your baby is here, you'll be overcome with joy."

Melanie didn't respond, she simply nodded. She knew her

mother meant well, but she wasn't sure how true that would be.

"Mrs. Ford?" Dr. Banks asked as she walked into the room and extended her hand out to Melanie.

"That's me and this is my mother, Mary Elle."

"Pleasure to meet you both," Dr. Banks said as she sat down and reviewed Melanie's file.

They got to hear the baby's heartbeat and cried tears of joy and the miracle of life that was taking place right before their eyes. The baby was growing strong and healthy and all was excellent with Melanie's health, too. Dr. Banks scheduled a sonogram and the next visit.

"Can you believe I'm going to be a grandma?" Mary Elle asked on their way back home.

"Can you believe I'm going to be a mom?" Melanie replied, and they broke out in a fit of giggles.

Maybe her mom was right. Hearing the baby's heartbeat had really put things into perspective. She'd known all this time she was growing a tiny human inside her, but hearing the heartbeat had made everything so much more real. She couldn't wait to hold the baby in her arms.

CHAPTER 4

The next morning, Melanie headed to the office before the sun came out. She was too excited to sleep. She jumped out of bed and got ready for work, careful to not wake Mary Elle. Melanie would meet her first clients today, and she wanted to make a good impression.

When she first moved to New York, she had started off as a photographer, but had leaped up the ladder to become the creative director for a women's magazine. Her first love had always been photography. She especially loved photographing weddings, engagement shoots, and family photo sessions.

"Good morning," Thomas said as he placed a blueberry muffin on her desk.

"Good morning! I didn't see you come in. How are you?"

"I'm doing pretty good. How are you?" He asked, eyeing her carefully.

"I'm okay, meeting my first clients today, and I wanted to get a head start. I have my portfolio ready but I also updated my social media accounts with some more recent work."

"That's fantastic. I was a little worried to see you here so early."

"Oh, I'm okay. Don't worry about me."

"I know you've got a lot going on right now, but I am glad to have you here. I have no doubt that you will be an amazing addition to our team."

"Thank you, Thomas." Melanie said and looked away as she started to tear up. These pregnancy hormones were really getting to her.

"I'll be around if you need anything." He said as he made his way out.

A few hours later, Mary Elle popped into Melanie's office with a clipboard in hand.

"Are you ready?" She asked.

Melanie took a deep breath and said, "let's go!" She didn't remember being so nervous about meeting clients before, but she really wanted to do a great job and make everyone at Willow Acres proud.

It had been a while since she had done a wedding or engagement shoot, so she hoped the clients would like her portfolio. As they approached the conference room, it surprised her to see Cade sitting there with a beautiful blonde.

"Cade! You're our client today? I didn't see your name on the questionnaire," she heard Mary Elle say.

Cade quickly stood up and said, "Yep, this is my fiancé Alana," but he couldn't keep a straight face, and Alana rolled her eyes and nudged him on the side with her elbow.

"I'm his sister. My fiancée couldn't make it today, so Cade is filling in for this meeting," Alana said.

"Cade, you're such a jokester," Mary Elle said with a giggle.

"I couldn't stop myself," he said, as his eyes sparkled playfully.

"Nice to meet you," Melanie said to Alana as she extended her hand out for her to shake.

"Thank you for seeing us on such short notice."

"The pleasure is all ours. We can't wait to help you plan your dream wedding," Mary Elle said as they all took their seats.

"Matt hasn't stopped talking about this place all summer. I'm excited to finally be here."

"Alana isn't much of a country girl so it's been very difficult getting her here." Matthew said as he appeared and took the seat next to Alana. She wasn't expecting him to attend this first meeting because of work.

"Yes, but I can see how much he loves this place and that it would mean a lot to him if we got married here." Alana said as she placed her hand on Matt's lap.

Matthew smiled sweetly at her, and Melanie felt a small tug in her chest. She wondered if she would ever share that look with anyone again. Melanie looked away, but caught Cade staring at her before he glanced away.

She cleared her throat and said, "We would love to have your wedding here. I am not much of a country girl myself, but Willow Acres has completely won me over."

"Melanie just moved here from New York City," Cade said, filling the couple in.

"Oh wow! That is such a big change. I can't imagine leaving New York to be here. What brought you here?" Alana said with a look on her face that Melanie couldn't quite place.

"I'm separating from my husband."

"Oh no, I'm so sorry. My brother is the best divorce attorney in town," Alana said giving Cade a nudge.

"I'm the only attorney in town," Cade reminded her.

"Doesn't mean you're not the best!" Alana said with a giggle.

"I'll reach out to you soon," Melanie said.

"So, we've prepared a small presentation for you to see events we've hosted here. After we go over the presentation, I would love to show you around the property," Mary Elle said, getting back to business.

Melanie had worked on the PowerPoint presentation and added some romantic music to animate it and excite the brides.

"I love the fall weddings you have hosted here," Alana said with a smile that didn't quite meet her eyes.

"We can fit a fall wedding for next year," Mary Elle said

"Oh, we were looking into a fall wedding this year," Alana said softly.

"We have about a month. I think we can do it. What do you think, Mom?" Melanie asked, looking at Mary Elle expectantly.

"I think it's possible. We have great relations with vendors and flowers and we can do catering in-house, if that's ok with you," Mary Elle said to Alana.

"I wouldn't mind that at all. I know it's short notice, but I think it's the perfect timing to get married," Alana said as she glanced over at Matt who smiled adoringly back at her.

"We will get started right away." Mary Elle said as she led them on a tour of Willow Acres to find the perfect spot for the ceremony, as Alana had stated she wanted an outdoor wedding.

While they were on a tour of Willow Acres with the happy couple and Cade, Melanie wandered off towards the stables. Melanie had always had a soft spot for horses. Growing up, The Black Beauty had been her favorite movie, and she had wanted a horse ever since.

A beautiful gray horse greeted her with a very excited neigh.

"Oh, hi there," she said as she reached out to pet the horse. "Aren't you just the cutest?"

"I see you made acquaintance with our big boy," she heard a voice say from behind her.

Melanie jumped at the sound of his voice and turned to face him, "Jasper, hey, I didn't hear you approaching."

Jasper smiled, and his green eyes twinkled with the sunlight. "It's ok. I haven't seen you around much since you started. How is Willow Heights treating you?"

"It's been amazing, so far. I thought it would take me a while to get used to the slower pace, but I love it, actually."

"This place had a way of making everyone fall in love with it. Once I visited here, I never wanted to leave. It's also the best place for starting over."

"That's exactly why I'm here." This was her clean slate from her past. All the memories that haunted and consumed her were slowly drifting away. Every day that passed by made her life in New York seem like a distant memory.

She took a deep breath of the crisp autumn air, and a sense of peace washed over her. This is where she belonged. She was safe here. No one would hurt her or her baby. This was home now. She and her baby would lead a peaceful life, and that was all she could ask for.

As she watched Jasper work, she reflected on how much her life had changed since she got here. She no longer had to attend fancy parties where she felt out. She didn't have to be fake in order to fit in. Melanie could be herself, and they accepted her just the way she was. Melanie had spent her whole life trying to find a place to call home. She never felt like Helena Springs was home and she thought escaping to New York City was what she needed, instead she had felt more alone there. Willow Heights felt like the place she had been searching for her whole life. Melanie truly felt like she was finally home in Willow Heights.

* * *

Dᴜʀɪɴɢ ʜᴇʀ ʟᴜɴᴄʜ ʙʀᴇᴀᴋ, her soon to be ex-mother-in-law called her again. Melanie didn't bother to answer. She knew it was just to rehash the past and talk about things she didn't care to talk about anymore. Again, no voicemail message was left, so it must not be an emergency. She knew Everett had already moved out of their apartment and was back at work. He didn't skip a beat. But that was fine with Melanie. She knew she didn't need him.

Melanie ate her lunch on the outdoor deck of the restaurant. She needed fresh air and to hear the birds and water to relax. She enjoyed her Italian sub sandwich with salt and vinegar chips in solitude. Sometimes she just needed to be alone.

She watched as Mary Elle and Thomas strolled by hand in hand and she couldn't help but smile. She loved seeing her mother so happy and finally receiving the love she deserves. Her father was a good man, but his true love had always been his business and it was never a secret to any of them: they were all second fiddle.

She was about to pack up and head back into the office when she saw Alana walk out of the main house. She was on a call and looked around cautiously but didn't spot Melanie.

"I can't do this anymore," Alana said to whoever she was on the phone with.

Melanie knew she should stop eavesdropping, but she couldn't help herself. Alana seemed really uncomfortable.

"I have to go. Bye," Alana said, and hung up the call.

She looked up, and her eyes locked with Melanie's.

"Sorry, I didn't see you there." Alana said as she walked over to her.

"I was finishing up my lunch. Is everything okay?"

"Yes, everything is okay. How are you? Cade told me you just moved here. How is that going?"

"Every day gets a little easier. You must be so excited about your big day," Melanie said, hoping to shift the attention off of her.

It probably wasn't a good idea to get into a discussion about her failing marriage with someone planning the happiest day of her life.

"Yeah," Alana said, not meeting Melanie's gaze.

"You don't seem very excited." Melanie wasn't one to pry into people's lives, but for some reason, she felt a connection with Alana earlier.

"Matty is such a good guy, and I know I won't ever find anyone else like him. I just can't shake this feeling that we're not a good match."

"Why? Have you talked to him about it?"

Melanie knew how Alana felt. She had felt that way before marrying Everett. She had often wished she would've talked to someone about it before jumping into such a quick marriage, but she knew now why she never had.

Melanie knew shortly after they'd gotten married that he wasn't the one. She hadn't brought up any of her concerns to her family or friends, because they would've talked her out of it. Melanie saw it clearly now, but back then, she was too proud to admit it. She was just happy to have met someone that shared her same love for photography and saw the talent she had.

"Oh, no. I couldn't break his heart. He is so good and I know I shouldn't complain because there are so many girls that could only wish to have someone like him, but we are so different. He wants to get married and move here and this place is great, but I can't see myself here. Plus, he's one of my brothers' best friends."

"Alana, you need to talk to him. Tell him how you feel. A

relationship will never work if you keep quiet about your needs and wants. By ignoring your own needs, you're not helping anyone, you'll only resent him. Matt is not a mind reader. I'm sure you can come into some sort of agreement."

"I met Matt shortly after a terrible break up. He was the perfect gentleman and treated me like a princess, but I never felt the butterflies. I never felt the way I did with my ex and I know I shouldn't complain or compare the two, but I feel like I would miss out on a lot if I picked Matt."

"Were you just on the phone with your ex right now?"

"Yes," Alana said, and tears quickly started streaming down her face, "I'm such a terrible person."

"You're not. It's normal to get cold feet before a wedding."

"Did you have cold feet before yours?"

"Yes."

"What happened?"

"I wish I wouldn't have gone through with it."

Alana nodded and quietly said, "I think I know what I need to do."

CHAPTER 5

*I*t had been a few days since Alana and Melanie had spoken. She heard from her mother that they had called the wedding off. Melanie felt terrible about that and felt like it was partly her fault.

Did what she say make Alana change her mind about Matt? He was such a great guy and Alana was a lovely girl. Surely, they could've made it work.

"So, today's couple will be here soon," Mary Elle said as she made her way into Melanie's office with her trusty clipboard in hand.

Melanie had helped Mary Elle come up with an intake form for all new clients with questions on their preferences for the wedding and the colors along with a brief paragraph on each couple's likes and dislikes.

Melanie looked down at her copy of the couple's intake form. They had sent it back by email the night before.

"It says there's only going to be six wedding guests, is that correct?" Melanie asked, looking up at Mary Elle.

"Yes, they are going for the elopement feel with only their kids as the guests."

Melanie knew from the intake form that the couple was in their 50s and they were very adventurous.

"Do you think they would like to get married by the overlook?"

"That would be amazing. The bride, Sarah, sent me some examples of what they're looking for and I saw a lot of mountain sunrise pictures."

"Seems like we have just the spot for that."

"She's going to love it!" Mary Elle said, as she excitedly jotted down ideas on her copy of the intake form.

"Have you heard from Cade?" Melanie asked her mother before she could stop herself.

Mary Elle looked up from her notes and said, "Thomas mentioned that he's very focused on some projects in the city, so we won't see him around for a while."

"I feel terrible about what happened." Melanie said as she nervously twisted her scrunchy around on her wrist.

She hadn't told her mother about her conversation with Alana; she felt guilty, and she wasn't sure if anyone would blame her about the breakup.

"Everything happens for a reason. I could tell during our walkthrough that Alana wasn't on the same page. It's better that she realized it now before the wedding. I'm sure it wasn't easy to walk away, but it shows strong character."

Melanie knew her mother was right, but she still blamed herself for what happened. Maybe she had projected her feelings on to Alana? After all, she was the last person who should give anyone relationship advice right now.

* * *

MELANIE SAT in the break room with her hands around a warm cup of tea. She usually liked to enjoy her lunch outside, but it had been raining all day, making it impossible to do so. She had three missed calls from her mother-in-law and an unheard voicemail, but she wasn't ready to cross that bridge yet. This was the third time this week that she called.

She knew she should take the call, but her relationship with her mother-in-law had never been the best. With what was going on with Everett right now, she didn't know what she could possibly talk to her about.

"Hi Mel," Molly said, poking her head into the break room.

"Hi Molly, what's up?"

"There's someone here to see you..." Molly said.

"Oh, I thought we didn't have any more clients coming in today," Melanie said, looking down at her smartwatch to check the time.

Suddenly the door that Molly had been standing behind burst open and Susan, Everetts mother, walked in.

"Susan, what are you doing here?" Melanie was stunned to see her ex-mother-in-law burst into the room. Susan and Melanie never had the best relationship, so she was sure this would not be a happy reunion.

"You haven't been answering my calls," Susan said, as she looked around the room. "I had to come all the way over here and ask everyone around about you until I found you. What were you thinking, running off and leaving my son all alone? And pregnant with his child!"

Melanie starred at her mother-in-law in disbelief. Is that what Everett told her happened?

"Could you please sit down so we can talk?" Melanie said, motioning to the seat in front of her.

Susan scuffed, but took the seat across from Melanie.

"Well? What is it you want to talk about then?"

"First of all, I am sorry I haven't been taking your calls," Melanie said as Susan rolled her eyes.

"Right. Well, explain to me what was going on in your mind when you left my son?"

Melanie took a deep breath. "I told Everett I was pregnant and he accused me of getting pregnant only to ruin his career, which..."

Susan's laughter cut her short. "My son would never say that."

"I have no reason to lie."

"And I have no reason to believe you."

Melanie sighed, pulled her phone out of her purse, and placed it in the middle of the table. She played the voicemail that Everett left her the day she told him she was pregnant.

In the message, he told her he never wanted to see her again and that he wanted nothing to do with the baby. After listening to his message, Melanie had gathered a few of her things and gotten on the first plane to Georgia.

Susan said nothing at first. She just sat there, staring at the phone. Melanie wasn't sure what she should do. Finally, Susan cleared her throat and Melanie's eyes met hers.

Susan opened her mouth as if to say something but then shut it again, "I've never been your biggest fan..."

Melanie sat there, in shock, not sure what to do. Was she really going to pin this on her?

"My son should know better than to react that way. I am sorry. I thought he had changed, but it seems he has taken after his father. Everett will change his mind, I can guarantee you that."

"Don't worry about it. He has made his choice very clear. I have no wish to be a burden on him. My baby will have everything it needs here and will lack nothing."

"I didn't want to bring this up before, but it wouldn't be surprise me if the baby isn't even his," Susan said, and left just as fast as she had come in.

Melanie sat there, speechless. She felt like someone had just slapped her.

David had been standing at the coffee machine and made his way over to her table.

"Are you okay?"

"I'm so sorry that you had to witness that. I didn't see you come in."

"Things seemed heated, and I didn't want to interrupt. Are you okay?"

She nodded her head. No looking back, only forward, she reminded herself.

"Never been better." She said, and she truly meant it. She thought facing Susan would be harder than this, but she was glad to have finally gotten this over with.

She was ready to move on from her past and to focus on her life and her baby. She couldn't wait to have her baby here and give it all the love she had to give.

"That's what I like to hear," David said as he gave her a wink and left the room with his coffee mug.

* * *

Mary Elle was putting the finishing touches on the charcuterie board she prepared for Melanie when she heard her coming in. She made flowers out of the salami and pepperoni and added various different types of cheese, fruits, and crackers, as well as honey. She heard through the grapevine that Everetts mother had paid Melanie a surprise visit. Mary Elle had never met Susan, but she knew she had never been quite fond of Melanie.

"You're home early," Melanie said as she sat on the kitchen Island and popped a grape into her mouth from the charcuterie board.

"I wanted to do something special for you. I heard you

had an unexpected visitor. How did it go?" Mary Elle asked as she joined Melanie.

"It went as well as expected. Honestly mom, I'm just ready to move forward."

"It makes me very happy to hear you say that. I worry so much about you."

"I guess you could say that you've inspired me," Melanie said with a shrug of her shoulders

"What do you mean?"

"When dad left you, we all expected you to fall apart. You had never really lived alone and your whole life had always been about us and dad. But look at you now mom, you're leading a great, fulfilling life and you found a love that most of us can only dream of."

Mary Elle felt her eyes fill with tears, "Honey, it wasn't easy, but I knew I wasn't helping anyone if I just wallowed in self-pity."

"I know, and I know it won't be easy. I'm well aware that there will be hard days, but I'm ready for what the future holds."

* * *

IT HAD BEEN a couple of weeks since Susan made an appearance. Things had been calm in Willow Acres since and Melanie was quickly finding a routine she enjoyed. She always felt that she worked best when she had a routine. It may be old school of her, but she still loved using planners to keep up with her tasks. There was something so satisfying about scratching items off of her to do list.

She had gone to her doctor's appointment after work today and was on her way back home when her car made a strange noise. While at the doctor's office, she had gotten a weather advisory notification on her phone, but she thought she had enough time to make it home before it hit. She looked around her car for an umbrella or a jacket but unfortunately didn't have one at hand.

The rain was coming down hard, and the road was barely visible. She pulled over to the side of the road and jumped off to see what was wrong.

"Oh no, please no!" she said when she noticed she had a flat tire. She glanced down at her phone, but she had no service. Just her luck. What was she going to do now?

It must have been her lucky day because after not seeing any other car for miles, here came a big black pickup truck.

"Hey!" she called out, waving her hands and the pickup truck slowed down once it got closer to her. She had listened to enough true crime podcasts to know this wasn't a great idea, but she felt like she had no choice.

The pickup truck came to a halt right in front of her, and the window rolled down slowly.

"Need some help?" Cade asked with that brilliant smile of his.

"Cade? Oh, thank goodness it's you! I have a flat tire and my car is also kind of stuck in the mud."

Cade had made his way over to her car and was inspecting the tire.

"Get in my car so you're out of the rain. Do you have a spare?"

"No, I don't." Melanie said and broke down in tears. It was silly to get worked up over something like this, but she felt so helpless in this moment. How was she going to make it as a single mother? If Cade hadn't shown up, who knows how long she would've been stuck there.

"Okay, that's ok." Cade said and Melanie could tell by the look on his face that he was coming up with a game plan. "Let's go to my house, its right around the corner. You can change into some dry clothes and we'll figure it out from there."

They turned onto a one lane dirt road with trees on either side. It was very dark, and the road was barely visible. She jumped at the sound of a loud thunder.

"Are you alright?" Cade asked

"Yeah, I've just never been a fan of thunder and lightning."

Thunderstorms had terrified her since a very young age. She would always climb into her parent's bed at the first sound of thunder.

"Really? I find them so fascinating."

Melanie didn't answer him because shortly after, a gorgeous 'A' frame cabin came into view.

"This is your house?" Melanie asked in awe. She'd only seen a place like this on social media. She didn't know anyone that actually lived in a place like this. With what she knew about Cade, this seemed like just the place that he would live in.

"Yep, David and I built it ourselves."

"It's gorgeous!" The front of the cabin was all glass windows and the roof that went down to the floor was black. There was also a large front deck with a very welcoming seating area. Melanie was so awestruck that she had completely forgotten about the thunderstorm.

"Thank you. I wanted it to be an investment property for short-term rentals, but once we were done, I couldn't give it up."

"I can see why," Melanie said, as she carefully got out of the truck. She was petite, and she felt like she needed a ladder to make it safely to the ground.

Cade invited Melanie in and offered her a dry t-shirt and a warm blanket. She still didn't have cellphone reception up in the cabin. Cade served her a warm cup of tea and prepared a small snack.

Melanie looked around the cabin and admired how tastefully done it was. It was rustic and cozy. Melanie called Mary Elle from the cabin's landline to let her know where she was and about the flat tire.

"Ok, I'm so glad Cade found you," Mary Elle said.

"He was nice enough to stop and help me. He's now looking for a spare tire in his shed," Melanie said.

Unfortunately, Cade didn't have any spare tires that would fit Melanie's car. He called David, and he offered to bring one up to the cabin.

As they waited for David to arrive, they made small talk and Cade gave her a tour of the cabin.

"This place is massive!" Melanie said as she looked around, amazed at the beautiful craftsmanship.

"It's three floors, and a finished basement."

They started off in the kitchen, which had black counters and concrete countertops and backsplash.

"A-frame cabins I've seen around are usually a lot like mountain cabins. This one is all cool and dark. I can totally tell that you designed it."

" You're right. I loved the idea of an A-frame cabin, but most of them have one little crammed bedroom and are basically just wood. Since we have so much land here, we really wanted to use that to our advantage. As I mentioned before, I originally wanted this to be an investment property, so I wanted it to be a place where groups could come and get away from it all. We wanted it to feel like a retreat and we definitely wanted it to be aesthetically pleasing."

Melanie had never heard Cade say so much in such a short amount of time. He usually sat back and observed, but she could tell this was his passion and true calling.

"You definitely built that here. I can definitely see all my influencer friends from the city coming here to get away from the hustle and bustle."

"Since I couldn't let this place go, we are building another one a few miles down the road."

"Is all this your land?"

"Yes, it's been in my family for many generations."

"That's amazing. I'm sure once you get the cabin ready, that will also bring in lots of tourists to Willow Acres."

"That was also a part of the plan."

Once they reached the basement, Melanie could tell that Cade's mood had shifted and she wasn't sure why.

"The basement has two bedrooms and a bathroom. This here was going to be a guest room for my mom."

"Was?"

"She passed away a few months ago."

"Oh, Cade! I'm so sorry."

"She was so excited to see this place, but she never got to."

"What happened?"

"Pancreatic cancer. Stage 4."

"I'm so sorry Cade. I can't even imagine what that must've been like."

"You always think you're going to have more time, you know? Sometimes I still have the urge to pick up the phone to check on her or to drive by her house. It still doesn't feel real that she's gone. It really messes you up, but it made me realize that life is too short. One day we're here and the next we're gone. Anyway, how have you been doing? I can't imagine that going through a divorce would be easy."

"Well, it hasn't been easy, but I'm moving forward. I'm just ready to close that chapter of my life," Melanie said, hoping they could move on to lighter topics. Cade was such a laid-back guy; she didn't want to overwhelm him with her drama.

"That's good Melanie. How are you liking Willow Heights? It's quite different from the big city."

"I love it, actually. It's been such a pleasant change. I

needed to slow down a bit. I feel like I'm actually experiencing life now, whereas before it was as if it was all a rush."

"Exactly, that's why I came back here. After my mom passed away, I broke off my relationship with my girlfriend because I realized that life was too short to not do what you love. Willow Heights might not be for everyone, but I love it here and can't imagine being anywhere else. My city friends all think I'm crazy for wanting something slower paced, but it's just like you said, as if we are just on autopilot but not actually living and enjoying the moment, the process of life."

"I know, and I want to feel alive. I want to enjoy things."

While in New York, Melanie's life was strictly made up of work and social gatherings. Which left her feeling empty inside. She knew there was more to life than work and meaningless social interactions. She always wanted more, but she didn't know what that more was.

While in New York, she had no alone time, let alone time in nature. She hadn't even heard birds chirping until she came to Willow Heights. Now she enjoyed sitting out on the deck listening to the sounds of nature as she enjoyed a warm cup of tea. She remembered going on many trips with friends while in college. They traveled all over the world and spent a lot of time in nature. Unfortunately, once she graduated College and joined the work force, she took no time off. She made a promise to herself to never let that happen anymore. She would make herself and her baby a priority above anything else and she would show her baby all the amazing things this world offered.

Once they finished the house tour, Cade and Melanie went to sit outside. Now that the rain had cleared, it seemed like the forest came alive. She could hear many frogs and other creatures happily chirping away.

"Hey!" David said as he pulled his car out front. He always

had a smile on his face and was ready to help, no matter the situation. Melanie loved that about him.

Having him around had made her move much smoother and less lonely. He often came by her office to make small talk when he noticed she might be feeling down. They also went on walks around Willow Acres discussing projects and talking about life. He had become a very great friend to her in the short amount of time that she'd been there.

"Hey!" Melanie and Cade both said back to him in unison.

"I found a spare tire. Let's go before it pours again."

"Melanie, you can stay here if you want until we come back with your car," Cade said.

"No, it's OK. I'll go with you guys. It's getting late and I should head back home now."

"Sounds good," David said as he was getting the spare tire out of his car and loading it onto Cade's truck.

Once they replaced the flat tire with the spare, and Melanie was on her way home. The guys went into town to get some wings and watch a basketball game at the bar.

She still didn't have signal on her phone, so she waited until getting home to talk to her mom. On her drive home, she noticed she had something in common with Cade.

They both wanted a new start in a place where they could live life freely. A place far away from everyone's expectations, Melanie realized that his break-up also brought him something good. He could move and do what he wanted, which was to live life.

She learned that sometimes things ended to push you to do the things you might have been too afraid to do before. Who said endings were supposed to be a bad thing, anyway? Maybe endings were only an introduction to a new chapter of life.

CHAPTER 6

*M*ary Elle planned to make a romantic dinner for Thomas tonight to celebrate that Willow Acres had closed the books this month in green. They were going on their fourth great month at the farm. She felt like it was finally time to celebrate. They had exceeded their goal by a lot.

She wanted to show Thomas how proud she was of him and all the hard work he had been putting into Willow Acres. She knew that Willow Acres wasn't just a job to him; it was his family's legacy, which is why he worked so hard to see it succeed.

Mary Elle went by the grocery store to get a few things that she was missing. She was planning on making him his favorite pork loin roast with cranberry sauce, with a side of asparagus, and mashed potatoes. Though he didn't look like it, Thomas could eat and she loved cooking for him. Acts of service is one of her love languages and nothing made her feel more fulfilled than doing little things for her loved ones she knew they would enjoy.

"Mary Elle, I was just thinking about you," Deborah said as she brought her cart to a stop next to Mary Elle's.

"Debbie, it's so good to see you! How have you been?" Mary Elle said as she pulled Deborah into an embrace.

Deborah was the town's doctor's wife and Mary Elle had helped Deborah plan an extravagant birthday party for him a few months ago at Willow Acres.

"I'm doing fantastic. I've been meaning to talk to you because my daughter is getting married and I wanted your help planning the wedding."

"Congratulations! I would love to help. Pass by Willow Acres whenever you'd like and we can begin planning."

"Well, she wants to get married at Winding Creek Ranch, but you'll still help, right?"

Mary Elle hadn't thought about planning events outside of Willow Acres. Would it upset Thomas? Was there an agreement with her employment to only host events for Willow Acres? Had she signed a non-compete agreement? She couldn't remember. Everything had happened so fast.

Winding Creek Ranch was in the next town over. She had never been there, but had heard great things. She would love to plan a wedding there, but she didn't want to step on anyone's toes.

Seeing that Mary Elle was conflicted, Deborah insisted, "Please Mary Elle, it would mean the world to me. I don't want anyone else but you planning this wedding."

Mary Elle smiled and said, "How could I ever say no? I would love to!"

Deborah let out a small cheer and pulled Mary Elle into a hug. "I must call Emily right now with this great news!" and quickly took off, leaving Mary Elle alone with her thoughts.

She felt like she should've run this by Thomas first, but planning events was what she loved to do. She had already let one man stop her from living her life on her own terms.

Would Thomas do the same? She didn't think so, but she couldn't shake the thought.

* * *

It was the day of the Willow Acres Family BBQ, and Melanie was setting up the tables with Patty while Dean and David worked the grills.

"I think things are going well between us. He's so handsome, isn't he?" Patty was saying as Cade appeared with a cooler and Melanie couldn't tear her eyes away from him.

He was wearing a plaid button-down shirt with the sleeves rolled up and jeans. He smiled when he saw her and their eyes locked.

Patty waved her hand in front of her face. "Earth to Melanie?"

"Sorry, what were you saying about Dean?"

"I think he's warming up to me."

"I thought you said he wasn't talking to you?"

"Well yeah, but that's only because he was busy with coming up with new menu items. You know how he gets..."

"Well, I'm glad things are looking up for you two"

"What about you?"

"What about me?"

"Any lucky guy in your life?"

Melanie didn't say anything. She simply laughed.

"What? You're pregnant but you can still date."

"Who would date a pregnant single mother?"

"Who wouldn't? You're a great catch and look at you! You're glowing."

"Thanks Patty. But I'm okay. I'm just focused on being the best mom for this little baby." Melanie said as she patted her baby bump.

"Well, Cade keeps glancing over here."

"Cade?" Melanie asked, and she felt her cheeks getting red, but she didn't dare to look over at him.

"He's really cute. It's too bad for him. I already had my eye on Dean when I met him."

Melanie shook her head and laughed. Patty was crazy about Dean, and for her sake, she hoped the feeling was mutual.

"Everyone should arrive soon," David said as he approached them.

"Hey David, what's the deal with Cade?" Patty asked, and Melanie felt her blush coming back.

"What do you mean?"

"Like is he single? Is he taken? Is he ready to mingle?"

"He's single."

"Oh, now that's good news."

"Why? Are you interested?"

"No. I'm taken by Dean, but I might know someone that is," she said and gave Melanie a wink when David wasn't looking.

"I didn't know you and Dean were finally an item."

"We're not, but we will be. Wait, is there a no dating policy at work?"

"No, I don't think so. As long as it doesn't affect your jobs. I don't think Thomas would mind."

"So, what else do you need help with?" Melanie asked, cutting in before Patty could bring Cade up again.

* * *

TIFFANY WAS LOOKING FORWARD to surprising Mary Elle and Melanie by showing up today. She had been feeling very homesick and when they mentioned the Willow Acres BBQ; she knew she couldn't miss it. She would have to drive back home today, but as long as she got to spend time with her family that was okay. Tiffany let herself in to her mother's house and found her in the kitchen with Thomas.

"Tiffany! You made it," Mary Elle said as she saw her walking in and her face instantly lit up.

"I really didn't want to miss it, so I changed my shift with my coworker. I've missed you." She said as she pulled her mother into a hug.

"I've missed you too, honey." Mary Elle said as she pushed Tiffanys hair behind her ear.

"How can I help?"

"Could you pull out the mac and cheese casserole from the oven and take it to Thomas' car?"

"Sure," she said and sprang into action, only stopping to give Thomas a quick hug. She truly had missed her mother and her home cooking. It was lonely in North Carolina without her family. Once she had graduated, most of her friends had all moved away, and it had been hard to stay in touch.

When they arrived at Willow Acres, Tiffany ran over to where Melanie and Patty were sitting.

"Hey girls!" She said as she approached them.

"Tiffany, Hey! I didn't expect to see you here," Melanie said as she tried to stand.

"Don't get up. It's okay. Look at you!"

"Isn't she radiating?" Patty said.

"She really is and your hair looks amazing, Mel." Tiffany said as she touched Melanie's hair.

"It must be the prenatal vitamins," Melanie said with a laugh.

"I think Dean's looking for me. I'll be right back!" Patty said as she quickly dashed over to Dean.

"So, tell me everything that happened with Susan. I can't believe she blamed you for leaving Everett and then said the baby was not even his?" Tiffany asked very upset.

Melanie had called her right after Susan left her office. How could that lady think that way of her sister? Did she know Melanie at all?

"Yeah, can you believe it? Then she just stormed off. Who does that?" Melanie said as she poured herself a cup of lemonade.

"I'm just glad you won't have to deal with them for much longer."

Melanie sighed and said, "Agreed. No one has ever insulted me like that before. But as they say 'what goes around, comes around; if there was any cheating it wasn't on my part."

"Anyway, let's change the subject. It's not worth stressing over. How is the baby?"

"The baby is great. Growing. I'm feeling my clothing getting tighter. But I'm not ready for full on maternity clothing. Most of it isn't cute or flattering,"

"We should go shopping while I'm here."

"Sounds like a plan. Have you heard from Michael?"

"Last I heard, he and his friends were going to Vegas for the weekend. I don't know how he can meet all these women and date them. I feel like he's spiraled since our parents' divorce. He was also asking mom about the holiday's this year."

"I'm definitely not spending Thanksgiving or Christmas without mom," Melanie said as she took a sip of lemonade.

"I was thinking the same thing. Michael will probably go to dad's for thanksgiving."

"It's ok, I'm sure mom will understand. We should invite Ruby for the holidays as well. We haven't spent time with her and she's always working and never really has time to unwind and enjoy herself."

"That's a great idea. I think she's been feeling a little down since her breakup."

"She can do better. I mentioned to mom recently that I would love for her to be with Michael."

That caught Tiffany off guard. "No. No way," she said.

"Why not? Ruby is an amazing girl."

"Oh, no doubt about that. I just don't think Michael is ready for someone like her."

"I guess you're right."

They spent the rest of the day mingling with the rest of the Willow Acres staff and families. They played different games like tug-o-war, potato sack race, and they even had an archery area. Tiffany's favorite part was helping Jasper in the petting zoo with the kids and taking the kids on pony rides.

* * *

LATER THAT DAY, Melanie laid exhausted on the sofa from the BBQ. She'd had a great time with everyone, but there was no denying the toll the pregnancy was having on her body.

"Hey pumpkin, how are you?" DeeAnn asked Melanie as she walked inside the house and hung up her purse and jacket on the coat rack before heading to the kitchen.

"I'm great. How are you? How's the school year going so far?"

"Well, it's good, just a little backed up with some grading. How was your appointment the other day? I feel terrible that we haven't had time to catch up." DeeAnn said from the kitchen.

Melanie struggled a little getting off the sofa and joined her in the kitchen. "It went very well. The baby is growing and moving in there."

"So, is it a girl or a boy?" DeeAnn asked as she took a seat at the kitchen island.

"I'm not sure yet. The doctor wrote it down and put it in an envelope. I didn't want to know without my mom there."

"That's so sweet."

"I feel like it's a boy, though. I've been having dreams about the baby and it's always a boy in my dreams."

"Are you going to tell Everett?"

"No, he was very clear he wanted nothing to do with the baby and basically asked me to leave and never come back."

"Sorry dear, I didn't mean to bring up such a sensitive subject."

"it's ok. I'm moving on and leaving all that in the past. Even today when Susan just appeared at work, I was ok with telling her the truth and letting it go."

"You are a brave girl."

"I've learned it from you and my mom. You both are very strong women."

"Where is your mother?"

"She stayed behind cleaning up after the BBQ. Are you hungry?" Melanie asked as she looked in the fridge, trying to figure out her next meal.

"I'm always hungry. Can't you tell?" DeeAnn said with a laugh.

"Oh, stop that. You look great!" Melanie said as she made a family sized garden salad.

She'd been craving salads and random fruits. She laughed at the thought the baby must be a vegetarian. Melanie loved her steak, but the baby didn't agree with it. Melanie served DeeAnn and herself some salad. They enjoyed it and for dessert, Melanie was craving a cold, juicy watermelon, which she had in the fridge ready to serve and eat.

When they finished with dessert, they went to sit out by the deck. Summer was ending and autumn was coming in. Which made the perfect weather for evening tea time outside by the lake.

DeeAnn had a Lithuanian friend that sent her this amazing, and delicious tea called the Forest fruit tea. It was so delicious and drinking it by the lake made their evenings magical. The fire pit was lit and the warmth and light made the night extra cozy.

This is what she was referring to when she told Cade she wanted to feel alive. This small moment was just perfect. She was enjoying time with DeeAnn, chatting and drinking a warm delicious tea that made her think of an enchanted forest with beautiful trees and flowers with a warm and delightful fire to keep them warm. It was perfect.

She felt at peace with herself and the world. There was no need to rush from one place to another. This is what she needed at this very moment.

DeeAnn went back inside, and Melanie stayed outside for a little longer. She was enjoying the fresh air and listening to the small waves of the lake. She felt a small nudge at her feet. It was Mittens. She also wanted to enjoy the warmth of the fire and listen to nature. Mittens jumped on the chair next to Melanie and winked at her. Melanie had learned that was the way cats sent air kisses to their family.

As bedtime arrived, she carried Mittens inside. After a quick shower, Melanie went to bed with a new baby book she found online. Melanie hadn't thought about the nursery she would need for the baby. Being six months pregnant was sinking in. She realized she had started her nesting phase. Mary Elle's house was big, but she didn't know if she could ask her mom if she could have the basement as her bedroom and nursery. Maybe she needed her own place. She made a mental note to contact a realtor tomorrow.

Being a first-time mom, she didn't want to be too far away from her mom or her job. She started checking for homes near Mary Elle's house. Being such a small community, homes were not abundant, but there were a few. She bookmarked the places she wanted to see in person to see if they would be a good match for her.

CHAPTER 7

$\mathcal{M}$ary Elle stopped by the bakery on her way to work on Monday to surprise everyone with donuts and different pastries. She was also there to pick up the cake for Melanie's gender reveal. The cake was either pink or blue inside, depending on what the baby's gender was.

She got a large to go box of their favorite pumpkin spice coffee. In celebration that fall was quickly approaching, the bakery released their pumpkin spice treats out a few weeks earlier.

"Need some help?" She heard a familiar voice ask.

"James, hi! How have you been?" Mary Elle asked, as he took the box of coffee and the bag of treats from her and held the door open.

"A little heartbroken still that Thomas stole you away from me, but the pain gets a little better every day." James said as they walked to her car together.

"Oh, James, you silly man!" Mary Elle said with a laugh and a little embarrassed that she was blushing. She had always enjoyed her time around James. He was a great hardworking man and maybe if she had met James first, things could've been different, but by the time they went on their first and only date, she was already smitten with Thomas.

James owned an antique shop on the town's square. Mary Elle met him when she first moved to Willow Acres and bought a few key pieces for her home. She preferred to buy older furniture that had character and was built to last. She also felt like it was better for the environment and more sustainable.

"I heard you're planning Emily's wedding. Debbie is so excited. She came by my shop yesterday and wouldn't stop going on about it."

Mary Elle's heart stopped. Did Thomas know? Would it upset him that she didn't tell him herself? She'd planned on telling him, but it was just never the right time.

"Are you okay?"

"Oh, I'm fine. I just remembered there was something I forgot to do. I'll see you around, James. Thanks for your help."

"Take care, Mary Elle. It's always great to see you."

"You too," Mary Elle said softly. She felt like she was going to be sick. She closed her eyes and said a quick prayer, "Please God, don't let Thomas know yet. Give me a chance to tell him."

Mary Elle didn't have much time to worry about Thomas, because just as she was getting into her car, she saw the man that had been at Wyatt's home. She was about to get back out of her car to follow him when her cellphone rang startling her.

When she glanced back, the man was nowhere to be seen. Who are you? She thought to herself. She hadn't talked to Wyatt at the BBQ because he hadn't made it. It wasn't like him to miss an event like that, and she hoped he was okay. Each passing day things got weirder with him.

First, he missed work without calling in and when David and Thomas showed up at his house, his mother said he wasn't feeling well and was sleeping. He had eventually shown up to work a few days after that, but he never gave an explanation and Thomas wasn't one to push.

CHAPTER 8

*D*avid took a seat across from Melanie for their daily morning meeting. Bailey from accounting had mentioned that there was a rumor going around that Melanie was secretly dating David, which Melanie thought was funny.

"Why are you smiling?" David asked her.

"Oh, nothing. I was just remembering a little office gossip I heard."

"What is it?"

"That we 're dating!" Melanie said with a devious smile.

"What? Who said that?"

"I'm not sure who started it, but I assured them it wasn't true."

"Small towns," David said with a shrug.

"So, tell me about today's client?"

David had invited today's clients over unexpectedly and they hadn't filled out an intake form yet.

"The client is a family friend that is interested in doing a sweet sixteen party for her granddaughter."

"Sounds fun." Melanie said.

"I know, right?" David said laughing, "she wants a chic gothic theme."

"Really? That's different. It will be fun to plan."

"Oh, I am excited about this one! All the fall colors." Mary Elle said as she entered the room and took a seat next to David.

"Yes, the birthday is around Halloween. I think that's why they want it dark and gothic."

"This is going to be very different from our usual. I can't wait to see what you come up with." Melanie said to her mother.

"This is definitely outside of my comfort zone," Mary Elle said.

"I can help you. One of my friends had a party with this theme. We can downsize it and make it more budget friendly. I'll do some mock ups to show them some ideas and we can go from there."

"Sounds good and I'll run it by my uncle." David said he headed out the door.

* * *

MELANIE REACHED out to her friend, Blake, in New York City. She read over her notes as she waited for him to answer.

"Melanie, what a surprise!"

"Hey Blake, how are you?"

"Everything's good Mel. How are you? I've been thinking a lot about you. Susan was badgering us to find you."

"Yeah, she found me. She paid me a visit. It was very unpleasant."

"Well, Everett has been playing the victim, which has helped him find sympathy with some of the female friends."

"Unbelievable. If only they knew what he's really like."

"I know, but you're better off without him."

"I am. The reason I called you was to see if you had any photographs and props left from the Halloween Gala you hosted."

"I do. I can send you some photos of what I have in my studio. If you can use any of the items, then I can send them via courier."

"Great, thanks Blake. I appreciate you."

"Not a problem. I'm glad to hear you're working and living life. Let me know if you ever decide to come visit us."

"Maybe you can come visit us and have the Willow Heights experience." Melanie said. She didn't think Blake would take her up on her offer, but it didn't hurt to invite him.

"You never know Mel. I might just take you up on your offer!"

Melanie felt accomplished. She had checked off one item from her to do list already. She was excited to meet the family that was planning this kind of party. It seemed out of the norm for Willow Heights.

* * *

MARY ELLE and Melanie had lunch at The Grit on the square. They both ordered the apple pecan chicken salad with a raspberry vinaigrette.

"I didn't see you last night or this morning before leaving. How is everything?

"I'm ok, sorry about that, honey. It was so late when I got home that I didn't want to wake you and I had an early morning today."

"I thought you were being a naughty girl and sneaking around with Thomas." Melanie said teasingly. She loved the relationship that she had with her mother and that they could joke around with each other. Her mom truly was her best friend.

Mary Elle giggled, "How are you feeling, Melanie?"

"I'm good, excited to meet today's client. I called my friend Blake, and he's sending me some photographs of the props we can use if the client likes them."

"Ok, please show me what Blake sends you so I can include it in the presentation. I've never had this kind of event. I'll be learning from you Mel."

"Mom, you're the event coordinator. We will work together and it'll be an exceptional event. I was also thinking about asking Britney to come by and do a vlog to give us free publicity. What do you think?"

"I think that's a wonderful idea. We can ask the client if they would be ok with it."

"Sure."

Melanie quickly emailed Britney, one of her closest friends, who was an influencer and food vlogger.

Brittney had visited Willow Acres last year and had written a very nice article on her experience. This gave them exposure, and they got several new clients and visitors that came to enjoy the meals and venue as much as Britney did.

Melanie also reached out to Tiffany, who was also very stylish and hip. Tiffany wrote some notes down and would also send her some samples she had done in her other internship back in Atlanta.

* * *

MELANIE WAS WORKING outside on a bench by the lake when Mary Elle came over to join her. It was nice and breezy today and she wanted to be outside to gather inspiration. She was in charge of setting up a photo area near the corn maze and sunflower field.

"It's such a beautiful day, " Mary Elle said as she interrupted Melanie's thoughts. Mary Elle was holding the cake that would reveal the baby's gender.

"Is that what I think it is?" Melanie asked.

"Sure is."

"I'm so nervous. Should we do this now?"

"Whenever you want."

"Okay, let's do it now. I'm so excited!"

Mary Elle placed the cake on the bench next to Melanie and handed her a knife. Melanie counted to three before she cut into the cake. As soon as the knife went into the cake, she saw a small glimpse of the color blue.

"It's a boy! I knew it!" She said with tears in her eyes as she pulled her mother into a hug.

"Oh, Melanie, I can't wait to meet this little man," Mary Elle said as she rubbed Melanie's belly.

Melanie wasn't sure how to bring it up to her mom that she was thinking of moving out. She didn't want to hurt her feelings or offend her. She decided to just tell her. Melanie wanted her to know before she went out and started looking at places.

"Mom, there's something I need to tell you."

"What is it sweetie?"

"I'm thinking of getting my own place."

"Oh, why?" Mary Elle asked, taking a seat next to Melanie.

"With the baby coming in a few months, I want to have the nursery setup and also have some space for myself and the things that are in storage. I want to have my own office, too. I know you've welcomed me into your home and I appreciate it and love it there so much, but I would like my own space." Melanie said and watched her mother's shoulders relax.

Mary Elle placed her hand over Melanie's and said, "I

understand. It's not a problem. Have you started looking at houses? Are you buying or leasing?"

"I was thinking about leasing, but then I figured buying is more sensible. It's time I started putting down roots. I was going to go look at some places in this area. Would you like to join me?" Melanie asked. She valued her mom's opinion and knew she would help guide her in making the correct choice.

"Of course, I would love to!" Mary Elle said with a big smile on her face. Melanie was glad she had included her in the decision. Having her mom's full support made her more comfortable with her decision.

"Some places need a little TLC, but nothing major. I hope I can find a place soon and get started. I have some money saved for the down payment and for materials should I need to make repairs."

"Do you have a contractor in mind to help you?"

"No, not yet. Do you know of any? What about realtors? I saw two online and they both seem nice. One is Mr. Robert Cofer, and the other is Ms. Alice Klein. Do you know them?"

Mary Elle had quickly made lots of friends and acquaintances in her short time in Willow Heights. She was the go-to person for Melanie whenever she needed to find people or places.

"I know them both. They are both great. It's the place that matters most. You need to see the house and see how you feel about it. If you can picture yourself in it. They are making a new apartment building near Main Street if you would rather have an apartment."

"No, I rather have a house with some land to have a nice backyard for the baby to play in and maybe get a puppy. Rita has been teaching me and sending me books and videos on how to grow plants and vegetables. I want to try it."

"Ok, you definitely need a house. I'm excited for you

Melanie. You deserve great things and they are coming. The best is yet to come, my sweet girl," Mary Elle said as she hugged Melanie and planted a huge kiss on her head.

"I love you mom."

"You know what? Thomas is very good with his hands, and he's been helping Cade with his cabins. I'm sure they can both help you with any repairs you'll need to make. David could also help if he's not too swamped with his work here."

"I can't believe I hadn't thought of them. I will ask Thomas for help once we find a place."

Melanie quickly sent a text to Ms. Klein to let her know she would like to look at houses this weekend. She wanted to take advantage of Tiffany's visit. She couldn't think of two better people to house hunting with than her mother and sister.

* * *

WHEN MELANIE RETURNED to her office to check her emails and work on ideas for the upcoming events, she noticed she had a missed call from Susan. There was no voicemail, so she didn't think to call her back. About an hour later, Susan walked into Melanie's office with Molly, the receptionist, trailing after her, mouthing out an apology. Melanie waved her off, reassuring her it was okay, and focused her attention on Susan.

"Melanie, I came to speak with you in person because I believe it's imperative for me to know with certainty if that child you are carrying is my grandchild. I know Everett wants nothing to do with the baby, but I would like to know if there's a child out there that is part of my family."

"What do you want Susan?"

"I would like you to take a paternity test."

"I have no reason to lie about this baby being fathered by

Everett. I don't want to impose my child on anyone. That's why when Everett was clear and certain he did not want to be a part of the baby's life or mine, I left and I don't plan on ever going back or asking for anything in return. We will finalize our divorce, and I expect nothing at all from Everett. Not for me or the baby."

"So, you won't take the test?" Susan asked while handing Melanie a flyer.

Melanie glanced down and realized the flyer was for a prenatal paternity test.

"It's insulting, to be honest, Susan. I have nothing to hide, but for your peace of mind, I will take the test. But that doesn't mean I'm asking for anything, nor am I allowing you to have any rights over the baby. Everett gave up all his parental rights and therefore you have no saying in how or where I raise my child. I will have my lawyer make sure you don't come near my child without my permission or consent."

"Very well, Melanie. I underestimated you. I look forward to having the test results soon."

Melanie wasn't afraid of her anymore. She wasn't holding back what was on her mind anymore. This is her child. Everett is the father and they can't take away from her what he gave away. Everett made it very clear that he was giving up his parental rights and Melanie could not and would not seek any alimony for the baby. Which was fine by her because she wanted nothing to do with him and she didn't want her baby growing up with someone that would resent it. Melanie knew Susan might not be aware of all the clauses Everett and his attorneys wrote in the divorce papers, so she would take the test for Susan's sake, but she was not in a rush to oblige. She placed her hands on her desk and took a deep breath. She knew her mom and aunt were right. It was no use getting worked up over Susan. Her only concern moving forward was rebuilding her life and being the best mom she could be.

* * *

"KNOCK KNOCK," said a familiar voice as Melanie was looking out her office window lost in thought and trying to go back to being at peace with herself.

"Cade, how are you?" Melanie said as she felt a rush come over her. Was it the pregnancy hormones, or did Cade look especially handsome today?

"I'm good, just stopped by to see how you were doing and if you got your tire fixed."

"I'm okay. Yes, I got the tire fixed. Thanks for helping me out the other day."

"No problem, that's what friends are for."

"Did you have time to review all the paperwork Everett's attorney sent over?"

"Yes, and I responded the way you asked me to. He cannot get near you or your baby. Everything will be okay."

"Thank you. What about his family? His mother has been coming around and demanded I take a paternity test."

"She really asked you to do that?"

"Yes."

"You don't have to do that. Like I told you, Everett signed his rights away. He wants nothing to do with the baby. The baby is yours alone. Since he signed his rights away, she also has no claim on your child. If you want me to draft something for her, I can."

"Thank you. I don't think we need to act right now. I haven't decided yet how I would feel about her being in the baby's life."

"Whenever you decide, let me know. I'm sorry she's making this more difficult for you."

"Thanks Cade. I really" She didn't get to finish because Dean appeared in her doorway.

"Hey Mel, Jasper wanted me to tell you the barn is ready to be photographed."

"Oh, thank you. I'll be right there." Melanie said. She turned to face Cade and continue on with her with her thank you but Cade walked towards her and took her hands in his.

"Mel, stop thanking me. It's not only my job to help you, but I also enjoy doing it. I never met your ex but I have a feeling he's doing you a favor even though he thinks he's hurting you."

"You're right. He thinks he's hurting me and the baby, but the truth is we will be better off."

"I'll walk you to the barn. I have a feeling David might be there and I need to talk to him about something."

"Ok, sure." Melanie said as she grabbed her camera gear.

"How are the cabins coming along?" She asked him on their way to the barn.

"We are almost finished with the interior, then we'll have to do the landscaping and painting on the outside."

"It's so great that you get to build them yourself."

He nodded and smiled and she caught a glimpse of a dimple she hadn't noticed before.

"It's a lot of work. Thomas and David have helped me out on the weekends. It's an exceptional feeling when you see the completed cabin and you know we built it with love and good intentions."

"I'll be looking at some houses today. I need my own place before the baby gets here. So far, the houses I've found need some repairs and upgrades. I'm hoping to find one with little need for repairs."

"My aunt is a realtor here in town. Her name is Alice Klein."

"That's actually the realtor I'll be meeting with this weekend. What a small town!" Melanie said, realizing that everyone must know each other, which used to terrify her before.

"Keep me posted in case you need any help with the house or anything"

"Thanks Cade. I appreciate that," Melanie said, smiling and hoping that she would need his help. What was going on with her lately? Must be the pregnancy hormones.

CHAPTER 9

*M*ary Elle had woken up early and started baking Tiffany's favorite orange and date muffins. She wanted to have them ready for them to enjoy with coffee before going out house hunting for Melanie. After preparing the muffins, she took a long relaxing shower and by the time she was done, it was still only 8am. Tiffany wouldn't be there until at least 10AM.

"You're up early," Melanie said as she came down the stairs.

"You're up late," Mary Elle said with a giggle. Melanie was known for waking up no later than 6 AM, even on the weekends.

"This baby seems to mess with my sleep schedule." Melanie said as she poured herself a glass of orange juice.

"Are you having a hard time falling asleep?"

"No, I'm having a hard time waking up."

"That's normal. Enjoy it while you can." Mary Elle said as she placed a couple of muffins on a plate for Melanie.

"Wow, mom! These are fantastic," Melanie said between bites.

"There's more," Mary Elle said, pointing to the stack of muffins.

Melanie's first trimester had been very trying with lots of morning sickness and not being able to keep any food down. She'd lost a lot of weight and the doctor told her she needed to gain some. He had even recommended she eat vanilla ice cream, which Mary Elle had found odd. Now that Melanie was feeling better and able to hold her food down, Mary Elle tried to feed her as often as possible.

There was a knock on the door that startled both of them.

"I'll get it," Mary Elle said as she motioned for Melanie to stay seated.

She checked her watch, and it was only 8:15. Who could come over so early? Tiffany never knocked because she knew the door was usually unlocked.

When she opened the door, she was in shock at who she found standing on her front porch.

"Bill? What are you doing here?"

Bill looked surprised to see Mary Elle. As if he wasn't the one that had shown up at her house unannounced.

"Bill?" Mary Elle said again.

"I'm here to see my daughter," He finally said.

"Who is it, mom?" Melanie called out from the kitchen.

Mary Elle moved to the side and let Bill walk in. He took his time making his way to the kitchen, looking at the pictures on the wall.

"Dad, I didn't know you were coming." Melanie said when she saw him.

"I wanted to surprise you, but I can leave if you all don't want me here."

Mary Elle and Melanie locked eyes. Mary Elle could tell that Melanie was just as confused as she was, but she didn't want to impede on her and her father's reunion. This was the first time that Melanie was seeing her father since before the divorce.

"Don't leave, Bill. I was just heading out to do some errands anyway," Mary Elle lied.

"Thank you," Bill said and Mary Elle saw a look cross his face that she couldn't quite place.

* * *

MELANIE STOOD STILL, unsure of what she should do. She hadn't seen her father in a really long time. She had spoken to him a few times after her separation, but that was it. Growing up, her father had rarely been around. He was always working and focused solely on his company's success. However, she knew he had provided them with everything they had ever needed growing up, and she didn't take that for granted. Still, she didn't know what to do now.

"You look great," he said as he took a step closer.

"Thank you," she said and began twirling her bracelet around the way she always did when she was uncomfortable.

"This is a nice place your mom has here."

"Why are you here, dad?" Melanie asked before she could stop herself. She had never been much for small talk, and she was still angry at her father for what he'd done to her mother. She thought she had forgiven him, but seeing him here now only brought the pain and confusion back up.

"I wanted to see you. Is that really so hard to believe?" Bill asked, and the vein on his forehead that popped out when he was upset made an appearance.

"Honestly, yes. You've never been around before and you've never really cared. So why now?"

"Maybe I realized I let my family down. Maybe I feel like it's finally time to make things right. You're having a baby Melanie and I would like to be a part of the baby's life."

Melanie couldn't believe what she was hearing. Was it possible that her father had a change of heart? Why was everyone that had never been interested in being a part of her life was suddenly interested in having a relationship with her child?

She studied her father as he stood in front of her with pleading eyes. He seemed much older now than she last remembered. His eyes had a haunted look in them that she hadn't seen before. She didn't know if her dad had truly changed or if he was just bluffing, but she knew what she felt like doing. Without saying a word, she stepped forward and hugged her father. They stood there quietly holding each other and soon they were both crying. She didn't know who started crying first or why, but they stayed there in each other's arms, consoling each other.

"I'm sorry," Bill said as he took a step back and held her at arm's length. "I'm sorry that I was never there before. I thought that by providing all the materialistic things you all needed, that would be enough. I'm sorry that I didn't realize what it truly meant to be a father until now."

* * *

MARY ELLE RETURNED HOME by noon and was surprised to see that Bill's car was still there. She was unsure of what to do and almost left again, but the front door opened and Tiffany spotted her.

Mary Elle stayed in her car as she watched Tiffany jog over. She unlocked the car door for her and Tiffany quickly jumped in.

"I've missed you," Tiffany said as soon as she was in the car.

"I've missed you more," Mary Elle said.

"So, Dad showing up must have been awkward."

"Did you know he was coming?"

"No, of course not. He's leaving soon, though."

And sure enough, just a few seconds later, Bill stepped out of the house, followed by Melanie.

Mary Elle took a deep breath and turned off her engine. She would act like an adult and face her ex-husband once again. Bill's face lit up when he saw her approaching and she got a sinking feeling in her stomach.

"Elle, this is such a lovely place you have here."

"Thank you."

"Can I have a hug?" Bill asked as he held his arms out.

Mary Elle felt all eyes on her and really wished she had stayed in her car or driven off when she'd seen that his car was still there.

She gingerly took a step forward and awkwardly hugged him.

"Hello ladies!" someone called out, and Mary Elle didn't need to turn around to see who it was. She quickly removed herself from Bill's arms and faced the man that hadn't broken her heart.

"Thomas! What are you doing here?"

"I'm here to paint the deck, remember?" He said as his eyes darted from Mary Elle to Bill.

"Right, I forgot. Let's go look at the deck," she said as she spun around on her heel and made her way to the back deck. Thomas followed close behind.

Mary Elle should've known that Thomas would show up soon. He regularly showed up unannounced to fix things here and there that he noticed needed fixing. That was one of Mary Elle's favorite things about him. He was always so thoughtful.

Once they reached the back deck, neither of them said a word. She knew she should say something. She should explain what he had walked in on, but she was still confused herself. Today had been such a whirlwind that she was still trying to process everything that had happened.

"What's going on?" Thomas finally said as he eyed her suspiciously.

She felt guilty even though she knew she shouldn't. She had done nothing wrong.

"What do you mean?"

"Why are you acting all weird and why did I find you in another man's arms? Who is he?"

"Thats my ex-husband."

"Are you getting back together?"

Mary Elle broke out into a laugh; it was an undesirable trait she had. Whenever she was nervous, she would laugh and she couldn't stop herself.

Thomas stood there, staring at her.

"No, of course not," Mary Elle said as she took a step towards Thomas. "He came to check on Melanie. No one even knew he was coming."

"So, he's not here to take my lovely lady?"

"No."

"Good, because I have a feeling that many people would miss you if you left."

"You think so?" Mary Elle asked as she put her arms around his neck.

"I know so."

Mary Elle loved the way Thomas made her feel. She knew that there was no place she would rather be than in Willow Heights with him. Seeing Bill here had only cemented that feeling for her. She knew she never wanted to feel the way she had felt when she was with Bill. She'd never known what she was missing then, she never knew it until she met Thomas. Mary Elle knew she was complete as a person on her own, but being with Thomas felt like home.

* * *

THE WEEKEND HAD BEEN UNEXPECTEDLY MORE stressful than Melanie had liked. She was glad when Monday came around and she was back in her usual routine. She'd found a house that she loved and that Mary Elle and Tiffany had approved of. Her realtor had quickly gotten in touch with the seller's realtor and sent in an offer. Melanie kept checking on her phone to see if her realtor had called or texted. Unfortunately, it was almost lunchtime, and she still hadn't heard from her, which was doing nothing for her nerves or productivity at work. It didn't help that her aunt had tagged along today.

"I still can't believe that Bill popped out of nowhere and no one thought to wake me."

"We all know how much you value your beauty sleep."

"A girl needs her beauty sleep, but this was my one chance to tell him all I've been wanting to say," DeeAnn said as she popped a skittle in her mouth, "I just hope that if there's ever a fire someone will remember I live there too and wake me up."

"To be honest, my dad didn't seem like himself, so it was probably not the best time to get on his case."

"What do you mean? Do you think he and Barb are over?"

"I'm not sure. I didn't ask and I'm sure Michael or Tiffany would've mentioned it if they were broken up. He just seemed older and down."

"Well, I guess time will tell what's going on with him."

"Yeah, maybe it's nothing. But I do have to get some work done today."

"Maybe I can help you?"

"Do you know how to use the photo editing program, Lightroom?"

"Yeah, I know how to turn a light switch on."

"Aunt D." Melanie said sternly.

"Ok, I get it. I'll get out of your hair."

"I love you..." Melanie said apologetically.

"I know." DeeAnn said and blew her an air kiss as she walked out.

"I'll look around for you, so we can have lunch together!" Melanie called out after her.

Shortly after, the door closed behind DeeAnn; Melanie found herself alone in her office. She checked her phone one more time, but still no sign of her realtor, and she got a sinking feeling in her belly. She wished she hadn't gotten her hopes up, but she had fallen in love with that house as soon as she saw it.

Melanie had spent the whole night thinking of all the things she wanted to do to make it her own. Why didn't she never learn from her past mistakes? Here she was again, getting ahead of herself, only to be let down again. She put her phone away in her top drawer, so she wouldn't be tempted to keep checking it.

* * *

DeeAnn took a seat on the Adirondack chairs by the overlook. This was her favorite view in all of Willow Heights. She always liked to come out here when she visited Willow Acres. Today she needed some extra alone time out here.

She hadn't been feeling much like herself lately, which is why she had taken the day off. Moving to Willow Heights and being around her sister and her family had woken feelings inside her she had buried many years ago.

DeeAnn convinced herself many years ago that she didn't want kids. After dealing with other people's kids all day, the last thing she wanted was to go home and have to deal with more kids. But maybe her mother had been right all along? Maybe it was different when they were your own kids. Now, it was too late for her. Not to mention that she hadn't had a man in her life for many years either, and she missed that, too.

"Hey, you're back," Thomas said, cutting into DeeAnn's thoughts.

He was drenched in sweat from working out on the field all morning.

"Back? I've been here all day," DeeAnn said, unsure of what Thomas was talking about.

"Oh? I thought Mary Elle said she had some errands to run with you this morning and she would come in late today. Maybe she meant Melanie," Thomas said with a shrug of his shoulders.

"Melanie has been here all morning too," DeeAnn said, confused. Was the sun affecting Thomas?

"Hmph," Thomas said and walked away without another word.

That was weird, DeeAnn thought. Come to think of it, she hadn't seen Mary Elle all day. What was she up to? Had she lied to Thomas? Mary Elle wouldn't do that; it must just be a misunderstanding, DeeAnn figured.

MARY ELLE WAS on an emotional high from her meeting with Debbie and her daughter, Emily. Since Emily was Debbie's only child, they wanted to go all out. The groom was also an only child and his parents agreed that there shouldn't be a budget for their special day.

Mary Elle had never planned an event that didn't have any restrictions budget wise and by the looks of it both families wanted something extravagant. This would be a first for

Mary Elle, and she was both nervous and excited. She hoped she could pull this off and make both of the families happy.

She was happy to learn that the couple decided they were still going to use Willow Acres for the food, cake, and flowers, and she couldn't wait to tell Thomas. They would set up a meeting in a few weeks when the couple was back in town to do some tastings. She hadn't talked to Thomas about planning this and she felt guilty about having fibbed this morning, but she didn't want to get into it over a phone call. She wanted to wait to get into the office and talk to him face to face.

"Hi there, Molly," Mary Elle said as she clocked in for the day.

Molly looked up from her cellphone that she had been sneakily texting from and said, "Hi Mary Elle. How are you today?"

Mary Elle smiled as she watched Molly tucking her cellphone under some papers. She thought it was cute that Molly tried to hide her texting. No one at Willow Acres would ever get on her case over it; as long as she kept up with her duties, which she did. Willow Acres probably had the most laid-back work environment.

Thomas made it a point to make everyone there feel like family, and he called no one out. If anyone wasn't living up to their expectations, he would meet with them quietly and help them in that area.

"I'm okay Molly. How are you? How's your family?" Mary Elle asked as she hung her jacket on the coat rack.

"I'm okay. My family is great. My grandfather got discharged, and the doctor said he should just watch his diet." Mollys grandfather had been hospitalized last week because his sugar had gotten too high.

"I'm happy to hear that! It must be such a relief for your mother."

Her mother watched over her grandparents and also worked two jobs. Molly took the job at Willow Acres to help her out. She was only 18 years old and was taking a year off before starting college.

"It is. Oh, I almost forgot. She says thank you for the casserole. It was delicious, and I have your Pyrex in the break room."

Though Mary Elle had never met Molly's mother, Casandra, she had a soft spot for her. She knew she had a lot on her plate and when Molly's grandfather was hospitalized, Mary Elle prepared some food for them and dropped it off on their doorstep, hoping that would relieve some pressure off of Molly's mom by not having to worry about cooking.

"I'm happy you all enjoyed it. Have you seen Thomas?"

"Yes, he was out in the field collecting the apples."

"Thanks Molly! See you around."

"See you," Molly said with a small wave.

MARY ELLE WENT to her office for a few minutes to catch up on emails and put the rest of her things away. Once she was all caught up, she went out in search of Thomas. She jumped onto her golf cart and made her way over.

She remembered Thomas telling her that with fall approaching, the apple pie had quickly become the most popular item on the menu. Thankfully, they had plenty of apples to pick, and they were ripe and ready.

Mary Elle's heart skipped a beat once she saw him. She couldn't wait to tell him about Emily's wedding.

"Hi Honey," Mary Elle said as she walked over to Thomas and handed him his stainless-steel water bottle. She noticed he had left it behind in the kitchen and had refilled it for him.

"Thank you," Thomas said without looking at her and guzzled all the water down.

"Is something wrong?" Mary Elle asked as she studied him. It wasn't like him to not acknowledge her with a kiss or a hug.

"No. Just trying to get some work done," Thomas said and walked away, leaving Mary Elle alone and confused.

What was going on with Thomas? He was being so cold. She wasn't used to this side of him. Bill had always been this way when he was stressed with work, but not Thomas. This was coming out of nowhere.

On her way back to the office, she saw Melanie and DeeAnn having lunch.

"Hey mom!" Melanie said waving her over.

Mary Elle left her golf cart in the shade and went over to them.

"Hi there, what are you two having?"

"I'm having some vegetable lasagna with a glass of milk and DeeAnn's having a salad."

"Can't get enough of this blueberry and blue cheese salad." DeeAnn said as she put a fork full of greens into her mouth. Mary Elle loved that salad too. Dean made his own mixed fruit vinaigrette that was to die for.

"Pasta with milk?" Mary Elle asked, scrunching up her nose as she looked over to Melanie.

"I know! It's gross and I would normally never eat this, but it's what the baby wants." Melanie said as she lovingly glanced down at her baby bump.

Mary Elle was so happy to see how far Melanie had come since she first showed up on her doorstep after leaving Everett. She was glowing, and she was genuinely happy. There was nothing that Mary Elle loved more than seeing her kids in a good place emotionally.

"What are you doing here?" She asked DeeAnn, concern all over her voice. DeeAnn never missed work.

"I took the day off," DeeAnn said with a shrug.

Suddenly it all came together for Mary Elle.

"Has Thomas seen you?"

"Yes,"

"I've got to go!" Mary Elle said as she jumped onto her golf cart again and went in search of Thomas. No wonder he was upset with her. He knew she had lied. She had to find him and explain everything to him right away.

* * *

MARY ELLE DIDN'T ENJOY HAVING any secrets, especially with people close to her like Thomas. She knew she had to find Thomas. She should've told him long ago, but she kept talking herself out of it. Mary Elle went back to where she'd last seen him.

She found Thomas gathering the baskets with Jasper and Billy.

"Thomas, can I speak with you, please?"

Thomas looked over to her and then over his shoulder at the others before saying, "I'm kind of in the middle of something."

"I know, but this is important and can't wait."

"Alright, give me a minute. I'll meet you in your golf cart."

Mary Elle could tell that his mood had changed from this morning. He didn't seem as upset. This made her hopeful.

Once they were in the golf cart, Mary Elle took a deep breath before looking into Thomas' eyes and telling him, "Thomas, I came to explain why I lied to you. I'm really sorry, it wasn't my intention for you to find out before I had time to explain everything."

Thomas said nothing. He only nodded, encouraging her to go on.

"I lied about this morning because I didn't know how you would react about me planning an event for clients that don't want to use Willow Acres as the venue."

Thomas looked at her with relief and said, "Oh, I thought you might have snuck some time with Bill or something."

That comment completely surprised Mary Elle. Why in the world would Thomas think she was sneaking around with Bill?

"No, that's definitely not happening. I ran into Debbie at the grocery store a few days ago and she asked me to plan her daughter's wedding, but she said she didn't want to use Willow Acres as the venue. I was debating how to tell you. Meanwhile, I met with Debbie and Emily today and they said they will not use Willow Acres as their venue for the wedding but will use our catering and photography services."

"Mary Elle, why did you ever feel the need to hide this from me?" Thomas asked and Mary Elle could hear the hurt in his voice.

"I'm sorry. I should've known better than to worry about how you would react, especially when you've been nothing but supportive since the moment you met me."

"Promise me you won't ever hide anything from me. I'm always open to hear your thoughts. I wouldn't have had any issue with the client wanting to use another venue for their wedding. You are a consultant and you can freelance. I want you to thrive and do what you love to do. I cannot and will not stand in your way."

"I just didn't want to hurt your feelings or step on your toes."

"You don't and I have to apologize to you as well, Mary Elle. I thought something was going on with you and Bill. It took me aback when I saw him at your house. You hadn't told me he was coming over and I assumed it was because you were hiding it from me."

"No, I did not know he was visiting Melanie. He had mentioned he was going to make time to come visit her about three months ago, but never showed up. I assumed it was typical Bill, always saying things he would do with the family but never doing them, so I honestly figured he wasn't ever going to make time for Melanie."

"I'm very sorry that I jumped to the worst conclusions because of what I've gone through in the past."

"Me too. I was afraid of how you would react because of the way Bill always did, but you're two completely different people. Thank you for hearing me out. I don't want to ruin things between us or have any secrets again. I promise to be honest with you."

"So do I, Mary Elle."

After they cleared everything up, they got back into work mode. Thomas went off to the apple orchard and Mary Elle went back to the office. She felt a great sense of relief to have opened up and been honest with him. She never wanted to be in a relationship where she couldn't speak up for fear of upsetting her partner.

* * *

MELANIE AND DEEANN were having lunch by the lake, but Melanie couldn't help but feel like something was bothering her aunt. Usually, DeeAnn always had a carefree attitude which showed in everything she did. However, lately she had been silent and pensive, which was nothing like her.

"Aunt D, what's going on with you? Are you ok?" Melanie asked.

"Yes, I've just been thinking about things lately. I guess

like an evaluation of my life and choices I've made.", DeeAnn said as she moved her salad around with a fork.

"Is everything alright? Anything you want to talk about?"

"When I was your age, I decided I didn't want to have kids. Being a teacher is my passion. I love kids. I just never felt like I could be a mother. Now that I'm older, I think I might have missed an amazing opportunity. I'm feeling lonely. It's not the same loneliness as wanting to have a partner, but more of like wanting to have a child to take care of and love. Maybe it's being around your mother and seeing all the love you guys share that has me feeling like I'm missing out on that."

"I understand. A lot of my friends are like that. They don't want kids, because they don't want the hassle and some just don't like children. There are many ways you can be a mother. You're still young enough to get pregnant and have a child. You can also adopt or foster children. Who knows, maybe you fall in love with a man that has his own kids and become their stepmother."

"You're right. I hadn't thought about many of those possibilities," DeeAnn looked at the time on her watch and said, "Gotta go, I'm going to be late to my horse-riding lesson with Jasper."

"Have fun!" Melanie called out after her and made her way back to her office.

She found a small bouquet on her desk. There was no card, but the flowers were beautiful and smelled divine. The arraignment was a delicate mixture of sunflowers, autumnal hydrangeas, pepper tree berries, dahlias, seeded eucalyptus, golden garden roses, privet berries, white roses, and bunny tail grass. It was perfect for autumn and romantic. She did not know who they were from. No one had ever sent her flowers before.

"Hey mom, did you leave some flowers in my office?"

Melanie asked Mary Elle as she walked into her office. Mary Elle was having tea and going over her Rolodex finding business cards for the venue Debbie wanted to use.

"No, honey, those aren't from me and I haven't seen anyone come by," Mary Elle said without glancing up, but Melanie could see that she was trying to hide a smile.

"Are you sure you don't know where they came from?"

"Nope, no clue," Mary Elle said, still not meeting Melanie's gaze.

"Hmm," Melanie said as she stepped out of her mother's office, not fully convinced that she was telling the truth.

Patty appeared a few minutes later with some baked goodies.

"Wow, those are some beautiful flowers!" She said as she placed the muffins and coffees on Melanie's desk.

"I have no idea who left them on my desk. Maybe they got the wrong office?"

"Was there a card?"

"No, nothing, just the flowers." Melanie said confused and wondering why they were left at her desk.

"Why don't you ask Molly?" Patty suggested as she got comfortable on the seat across from Melanie.

"I'll do that. I'm sure she saw whoever brought them. What did you bring? It smells so good."

"Dean is trying out many new recipes. Lisa is away this week, so he's in charge of the gift shop bakery. First is a decaf chai coffee for you and a caffeinated one for me because I need the caffeine," she said with a laugh, "We also have a ginger muffin with walnuts to share."

Melanie quickly took a bite of the muffin and a sip of the coffee. "Oh, this definitely hits the spot."

"Dean sure knows his way around the kitchen." Patty said with a proud smile on her face.

Melanie had observed the flirtatious banter that Patty and

Dean shared, but she did not know why they didn't pursue things. She didn't say anything because she didn't think it was her place, but she was sure they would make a lovely couple.

"Thank you for bringing this over. You really do spoil me," Melanie said with a genuine smile. Patty often came by with snacks for her and always made sure she had everything she needed. Melanie hadn't expected to grow so close to everyone at Willow Acres, but being here was exactly what she needed. She had friends back in New York, but apart from Brittney, she never felt particularly close to anyone else.

"Of course! I have to make sure that my little niece or nephew isn't missing out on all these fall goodies," Patty said before heading back out.

* * *

MARY ELLE still felt guilty about having lied to Thomas earlier. She really should've known better, and she felt terrible about it. Thomas had been lied to many times before during his marriage with Clarice. Of course, he would jump to the worst conclusions.

Mary Elle made it a plan to never lie to him again and to always be upfront with him. Thomas wasn't anything like Bill, and she had to stop treating him that way. She glanced at the time on her desktop computer and it was 30 past 5 pm. If she left now, she would have time to pass by the shop to get some things to make a nice dinner for Thomas.

He had a lot going on with the expansion of Willow Acres, and she knew he was still worried about Wyatt. Wyatt asked for a leave of absence stating that he needed to go take care of his grandmother, but they didn't really believe that was the real reason he was leaving. She hoped they could talk to him before he would leave at the end of the month.

"Hello?" she heard someone call out. Most of the staff had already clocked out for the day. Who could be out there?

"Yes?" Mary Elle asked, poking her head out of her office.

"Hi Mary Elle, is Melanie around? I passed by your house but no one was home and I have some exciting news to share." Mrs. Klein, Melanie's realtor, said.

"Ann, it's so good to see you. She's out by the pumpkin patch taking pictures. She's been waiting for your call all day."

"Yes, I feel terrible about keeping her waiting but I lost my phone and hadn't been able to get ahold of her."

"I heard. Cade came by earlier and told me. Here," Mary Elle said, digging into her pocket and handing a tiny envelope over to Mrs. Klein, "Please give this to Melanie when you see her. Cade came by earlier with a gorgeous floral arraignment, but we thought you should be the first to tell her about the house. I'll show you where the pumpkin patch is but I need to get going."

* * *

MELANIE TOOK a brief break to stretch her back. The pregnancy was making work a lot harder now. She had constant back pain and swollen feet, but she didn't want to stop working just yet. Melanie wanted to enjoy her maternity leave with her baby for as long as possible.

She was working late today because she had a doctor's appointment in the morning and was going to have to come in late. Melanie didn't mind working late. She loved how serene the evenings were.

"Hi Melanie," said a soft voice from behind. Melanie quickly turned.

"Hi Mrs. Klein, is everything okay?" Melanie said, a little confused, unsure of why Mrs. Klein was here.

"Yes, everything's fine. I came to see you because I have great news for you. They accepted the offer you made on the house and we will begin the closing soon, but we first have to do the home inspection. The seller is very excited and very motivated to sell.""

"Wow, that's amazing! I thought for sure we had missed out on the house."

"I'm sorry it took me so long to let you know. I lost my phone and didn't have time to come around until now. "

"It's ok. Thank you for coming all the way out here. Who are the owners? Anyone I might know?"

"You might know them. The owner is Chief Underwood. As you know, he is retiring and moving to be closer to family. The house you are buying is his childhood home. He kept it for as long as he could but he never got around to doing much with it and now that he'll be in Texas, it just makes sense to sell it."

"I'll take good care of it."

"I know you will." Mrs. Klein said as she looked down at her notepad and flipped a couple of pages before saying, "The inspection is next week and if all goes well and we don't need to negotiate, we can proceed with the closing."

"Oh, I almost forgot, this is for you. It belongs to the flowers you received earlier," Mrs. Klein said as she gave Melanie the small envelope.

"Thank you." Melanie said, placing the small envelope in her back pocket. It was drizzling now, and she quickly began to pack up her things.

"Here, let me help you."

"No, it's ok. I got it. I don't want you getting wet, Mrs. Klein."

"Don't worry about me. You're the one we should take care of right now," Mrs. Klein said as she quickly gathered things together and placed them in the basket Melanie had brought them in.

As they made their way back to the main building, Mrs. Klein said, "I will call you next week. I'm so excited for you!"

"I cannot wait! Thanks for all your help." Melanie said.

It wasn't until Melanie was getting into bed that she remembered the small envelope Mrs. Klein had given her. She got out of bed and dug through her jean pocket until she found it. She quickly opened it and read the message. It read, "Congratulations on the new house, neighbor." And it was signed by Cade. She felt her chest warm at the thought of Cade picking out those flowers for her.

She quickly grabbed her phone and texted him to thank him for the flowers. As soon as she sent out the text, she noticed how late it was and regretted texting him so late. A few seconds later, her phone dinged with a message from Cade. They texted back and forth for a little while and for the first time in a long time, Melanie went to sleep with a smile on her face.

CHAPTER 10

*N*ow standing in the living room in her new home, Melanie writes down a list of all the things she needs to address. The last few weeks couldn't pass by fast enough for her.

All she wanted was to begin work in her new home. With the baby due in only a couple months, she wanted the house to be complete by then. A light knock on the door takes her away from her list.

"Welcome to my new house!" She says as she holds the door open for Thomas and Cade.

"Nice place," Thomas says as he steps in.

"I remember when Chief Underwood's son Kenny used to live here. We always used to gather here to watch the games. You did good, Mel." Cade said.

"It needs some work but I cannot wait to make it my own."

"What have you got in mind?" Thomas asked as he rejoined them.

Melanie picked up her notebook again and began reading out the various projects she had in mind.

"That's all possible," Cade said, already planning what they would tackle first. "We can start working on it this weekend. I have some leftover wood and materials."

"That would be great!" Melanie said, full of excitement.

"We should start with the kitchen. That's an extensive project," Thomas said as he read over the list.

Melanie's vision for the house wasn't too extravagant. Instead, it was to modernize the kitchen and make the rest of the house cozy and kid friendly. Melanie had some counter-tops in mind and was waiting to get the measurements to place her order. She also had picked out fresh tiles for the bathroom and paint colors for the entire house. She wanted to fix the backyard, but she knew the best person for that would be Rita. Rita loved plants and was very great with landscaping.

After meeting with Thomas and Cade, Melanie called Tiffany. She would come down on the weekend to help her paint the house and shop for the minor things like door-knobs, décor, and new cutlery. Melanie's baby was due by Thanksgiving, so work had to be done rather quickly. Melanie wanted to get the house ready for the baby, so she made some changes to her wish list and concentrated on the essential parts that needed renovation, after the baby was born, she would focus on the rest of her list and take it slow.

ON HER DRIVE back to Mary Elle's house, Melanie received an unexpected call. It was Everett. Melanie didn't bother to answer the call. If it was important, he could leave a message. She continued to drive, and then there was a second call.

As she walked into the house, Mary Elle greeted her with her favorite pregnancy dinner: homemade cheeseburger with extra pickles and sour grapes. The baby had a taste for sour things.

"Looks so delicious, mom!" Melanie said as she took in the food.

"Thanks honey, eat up," Mary Elle said as she poured Melanie freshly squeezed lemonade.

"How was your day?"

"Good, how did the meeting with Thomas and Cade go?"

"Great, they are working on the house this weekend."

"That's amazing. I hope it's not too much work and they can do it before the baby gets here."

"They said they would work on it quickly. Cade has some friends that will also help him. Guess who called me?"

"Who?"

"Everett, but I didn't answer his calls. I have nothing to talk to him about."

"That's odd. Why would he call? Did he leave any messages?"

"No. I'm understanding now how toxic our relationship was. It's better for both of us that we're not together anymore."

"Oh sweetie. I'm just happy to have you here and seeing you work through this."

"It was very difficult to admit what was going on. It was exhausting to keep up with the facade of being happy when inside, I felt so depressed and stuck. But seeing how you could move on after what happened with Dad gave me strength. You are my hero, Mom."

"Honey, you are the brave one. You have a baby on the way and you did what was right for you both. I don't think it would have been a good place for the baby to grow up seeing you two fight and feel so much frustration and anger."

"I did it for him, for my baby. He deserves the best."

"We are here to help you give him the best. Don't worry Melanie, the baby will be loved so much."

"When all this happened with Everett, I was closing myself to everyone. I didn't want anyone in my business, or life, but now I'm opening up little by little. I realize I don't want to be alone."

"You'll always have us, darling."

"Thank you. You guys are all I need."

* * *

THE NEXT DAY, Melanie was at work when Cade walked in and brought her some donuts and pickles. Everyone knew about the baby's craving for pickles.

"These are for you."

"Thanks Cade, that's very sweet of you. Have a seat."

"Actually, I was just passing by. I was on my way to lunch and thought of you, so I passed by to drop these off for you."

"That's so kind of you. Thank you!"

Suddenly, Everett walked into Melanie's office. Melanie's face turned pale. It was as if she had seen a ghost or something awful. By the look on Cade's face, she knew he had noticed the change in her demeanor.

"Are you ok, Melanie?"

"Yes, I'm fine. Cade, this is my ex-husband, Everett."

"Nice to meet you, I'm Cade."

"Likewise." Everett said with a straight face. The tension was so heavy and palpable that Melanie was grateful when Cade excused himself.

"Enjoy the treats. Call me if you need anything," he said with a sweet smile. Melanie couldn't help but smile back at Cade. His gesture had touched her in a very special way. No one had ever gone out of their way like that for her. Not a guy, anyway.

Cade stood there for a moment, not moving, and Melanie knew he was dreading leaving her with Everett. She gave him a reassuring smile to let him know she would be okay.

"Call me if you need anything," he said again before turning and walking away.

"What are you doing here?" Melanie asked as she turned to face Everett as soon as Cade had left her office.

"I called you and you didn't answer so I came to see you in person."

"Again, what are you doing here?"

"I wanted to see how you were doing."

"Why?" Melanie wasn't buying it. There had to be a reason he showed up here.

"I'm worried about you. My mom said she thought you seemed stressed being out here by yourself. I wanted to check in on you and our baby."

"Really? Well, I'm sorry your mom misinformed you. I'm doing just fine and my baby is doing great."

"Look Mel, I want to talk to you and clear the air. Are you available for lunch?"

"No, I'm not."

"Ok, what about dinner tonight?"

"I'll have to check my calendar."

"Ok, I'll stay in town as long as it takes for you to sit down with me and we can talk."

"Fine, let's sit down and talk now. The quicker you go back to your mom's house, the better." Melanie was upset and didn't mind being a little sassy.

She grabbed her cellphone and directed the way to the restaurant. She passed by Mary Elle's office, hoping she would see that she was with Everett. Mary Elle glanced up as they walked by her office and raised an eyebrow when she saw them passing by. Melanie was glad her plan had worked.

Wyatt sat them down at a table near the entrance and bar area at Melanie's request.

He then took their orders, but Melanie said she only wanted water. Everett ordered a tuna melt with fries and a diet coke.

"Melanie, I know you hate me and you have a right to feel that way about me. But after the divorce I realized I had been harsh and extremely insensitive toward you and our child."

Melanie tried her hardest not to roll her eyes at him. She wasn't sure why he was here or what he wanted from her, but she wasn't buying it.

She sighed before saying, "Everett, I don't know what you're getting at, but let me assure you I am well and capable of being a mother to my child. You gave up your parental rights and I'm not asking for money."

"I know Melanie, I get it. But maybe I was too quick to say I didn't want to be a part of the baby's life," he said as he looked down at his hands and his shoulders slumped.

"Things between us were not right for a long time. The baby was just added stress to the marriage."

"Ok, but I've changed now. Give me a chance and I'll prove it to you."

"I highly doubt that, Everett."

"Melanie, I'm just asking for a chance to be a part of the baby's life, that's all."

"I don't want to go down this road with you. Our relationship was extremely toxic."

"What are you going to do when our child asks where's dad? Are you going to tell them it's your fault that you didn't allow me into their life?"

Melanie didn't have time to answer because Wyatt reappeared with their drinks.

"The sandwich will be ready soon," he said as he sat down the beverages and walked away.

Mary Elle and Thomas walked into the restaurant and toward Melanie's table. Melanie felt her shoulders relax when she spotted them.

"Hi Everett," Mary Elle said with an unreadable look on her face.

"Hello Mary Elle, how are you?"

"I'm well, thank you. This is Thomas. He owns Willow Acres."

"Hello," Thomas said, extending his hand out to Everett.

"Hello Thomas, nice to meet you," Everett said as he shook his hand.

"Likewise, we'll be having lunch over there. Please let me know if there's anything I can help you with."

Everett nodded and said, "Thanks"

Melanie could see that Everett was trying really hard to act polite. She had countless memories of him constantly complaining about her family and how much he disliked spending time with them.

"I just want a chance, Mel. I love you and I want to be a part of this new life we created," he said and Melanie noticed that his voice cracked. Was he about to cry? What in the world was going on with him?

"According to your mother, this baby might not be yours. She asked me for a paternity test. Did she tell you that?"

"No, she didn't. I'm sorry she was asking for one. You know she's very untrusting."

"Yeah, that I know. Everett, I don't think it's a good idea for us to try again. Our marriage was already over, anyway."

"Let me prove it to you, Melanie. I came all the way down here to sit and talk to you. Let's fix things. I hate what I did to you and our marriage. I'll do whatever it takes."

Melanie didn't know what to say. She didn't think it was a good idea to open her heart to Everett again. It had taken a great deal for her to come to terms and close that chapter. She had forgiven him and all that he had said and done. She did it for her own healing, but something inside of her told her to be careful and not go down that path again.

But he made a point. What was she going to do when her baby asked about his dad? Would he blame her for not letting him be in his life? How would being brought up without a father affect him?

"Everett, I can tell you I want the best for you. I've forgiven you for all you said and did, but I'm not ready to trust or even think about getting back together. If you want to be in the baby's life, I can respect that and I can allow you some time with the baby, but I cannot promise you a future with us as a family."

"That's ok. I will take what I can get."

"Fine."

"When is the baby due?"

"The baby is due the week of Thanksgiving."

"That's right around the corner."

"Yes."

"Does Mary Elle have room in her house for you and the baby?"

"No, she doesn't, but I bought a house and I'm working on making some upgrades. It should be ready by the time the baby arrives."

"That's great. So, you really want to stay in Willow Heights and raise the baby here?"

"Yes, this feels like home."

"I guess I'll come down to visit more often."

"If you wish to."

"Who is the guy that brought you the treats?"

"He's a friend."

"He seemed friendly."

"People here are friendly."

"Here's the sandwich," Wyatt said as he placed the plate in front of Everett

"Thanks Wyatt," Melanie said

"I don't want to make things difficult, Melanie. I just want to reconnect."

"Yeah, you've said that a lot, Everett."

Melanie felt uncomfortable and couldn't wait to get back to her office and send Everett on his way.

"Well, we've talked. I have to go back to work."

"Ok, I guess I'll finish my sandwich and then go."

Melanie got up and left. She noticed Mary Elle and Thomas were monitoring her.

Shortly after she made it to her office, her mother showed up.

"Hey sweetheart, how are you feeling?" Mary Elle said as she handed Melanie an Italian sub with extra pickles and some chips, "I noticed you didn't have lunch."

"I don't know, mom. Seeing Everett again was bitter-sweet, I guess. He said he wants to get back together and be in the baby's life."

"How do you feel about that? What does your heart tell you?"

"Well, I realized I don't hate him anymore. I had already forgiven him for everything, but I know it's not right to get back together with him because of the baby. It's just not a good idea."

"What about him being a part of the baby's life?"

"I don't know either. I guess we can start with a friend-ship, but I'm not pursuing anything more than that."

"Ok, then it's just a friendship."

Melanie ate her lunch and enjoyed the donuts and pick-les. She knew she had gained pregnancy weight and was shocked that Everett hadn't mentioned it. She didn't mind the extra weight as long as her baby was healthy and growing. Nothing else mattered. She would lose the weight in time. Melanie knew there were so many reasons she shouldn't even contemplate a friendship with Everett, but she didn't want to be selfish. She knew her baby would need a father figure and even though she didn't believe Everett was the best role mode; he was the father and there was no one else to blame for that than herself.

A text from Cade came in that read: "I hope you're having a good day after all. I'm here if you need me." That simple message made her feel warm and fuzzy inside. She texted Cade back: Thank you for checking in on me with a smiley face.

Later on that same afternoon, Everett sent her some flowers. They didn't have the same impact on Melanie as the flowers from Cade had. Everett added a card that read: Thank you for sitting down with me. You're glowing, and your beauty is breathtaking.

Melanie was expecting to feel butterflies, but there was nothing when she read Everett's card. She texted Everett, a simple thank you. Everett didn't text her back, which was ok with her. She was used to him not texting her back.

CHAPTER 11

elanie went into town to get some groceries and pick up some essentials for her new house. She couldn't believe she was officially a home owner. She had bought items to decorate and make it her home. As she was shopping, she ran into Cade.

"Hi stranger," he said, smiling

"Hi, didn't expect to find you here."

"Well, I ran out of steak."

"Steak sounds nice. I came to pick up some essentials, too. I was going to take them over to the house."

"I was going to stop by to bring some materials over to start tomorrow. My friends will help Thomas and I on Sunday."

"Yeah, I can't believe the weekend is already here. Tiffany is arriving tomorrow morning. We'll be painting while you guys do the kitchen counters."

"Thomas dropped off the paint this afternoon. It's all in the shed. I'll help you set up tomorrow."

"Thanks. I really appreciate you and Thomas."

"No problem. We are here to help."

As Melanie was walking away, Cade caught up to her and said, "Would you like to have a coffee or dinner with me tonight?"

"Yeah, I'm up for dinner."

"Let me help you with your shopping and we can head out."

"I'd like that."

Cade helped Melanie find the essentials, like toilet paper, water bottles, cookies, cups, paper towel and some other snacks, to have handy while they worked this weekend.

"There's this little bistro over at the end of Main Street. They have fantastic pasta. I don't know if the baby likes pasta, but it's great."

Melanie felt butterflies when Cade mentioned the baby's appetite. He actually cared about the baby already. That was something that Melanie had decided the next person she opened her heart to would need to do: love the baby as his own.

"I think the baby would like to try the pasta place."

They walked down Main Street and were seated inside the little bistro. Their table was in the corner, the lights were low and there was a candlelit table. It was such a romantic setting.

"What can I get for you tonight?" The server asked as she appeared next to them.

"Hi Shirley, I'll have my usual. The shrimp scampi with a side salad and a glass of Chardonnay."

"I'll have the chicken parmesan pasta with a Ceasar side salad and sweet tea."

"Excellent choices. I'll be back with your drinks and some garlic knots."

"I love the ambience, very rustic and Italian. I can't believe I hadn't been here before."

"Yeah, Mr. Russo's family owns this place. This is the best Italian restaurant I've found."

Shirley placed the drinks and garlic knots on the table.

"You'll love the garlic knots, they are delicious."

Everything smelled delicious and eating with Cade was just nice. She enjoyed how easily the conversation flowed between them. Melanie enjoyed his company; he was a gentle person. It was a wonderful change.

She didn't want to compare Cade to Everett, but she couldn't help but notice the difference in their temperaments and how they made her feel so differently from each other.

Their meals came, and they ate as they shared memories of their childhoods and laughed at the jokes they shared. They ordered tiramisu for dessert; everything was exquisite.

After dinner, Cade and Melanie walked back to their cars on the other side of Main Street. The weather was chilly and Cade put his jacket over her shoulders. This was another gesture that melted Melanie's heart.

"I hope you enjoyed dinner," Cade said as he opened her car do for her.

"I did. Everything was wonderful. Thank you for bringing me out."

"It's ok. I know you had a rough week. I thought you might appreciate going out for a while."

"I did. I truly enjoyed myself."

"I'll see you tomorrow bright and early."

"Have a good night," Melanie said as she waved goodbye to Cade from her car window.

Melanie couldn't stop smiling all the way home.

"WHAT'S GOT you smiling so much?" Tiffany asked Melanie the next day as they were painting her bedroom at her new house.

"Cade took me out to dinner last night," Melanie said, trying hard to contain her excitement

Tiffany broke into a big smile and said, "Wait, like a date?"

"Remember, I told you I was going to go buy some items for this weekend? Well, I ran into Cade at the grocery store and he asked me if I wanted to go have dinner with him and so we did."

"How was it? Tell me everything!"

Melanie spent the next few minutes going over every detail of her outing with Cade and she felt like it transported her back to their teen years when they would stay up talking about their crushes.

"So, are you guys dating?" Tiffany asked with a sly smile.

"I don't know. It's a lot happening at once. Everett wants to be a part of the baby's life. He wants us to get back together, but I know that would be a big mistake. Our marriage was not a healthy relationship and the love I had for him is not there anymore."

"Yeah, we all saw how he treated you. You deserve so much more, Mel. The baby deserves to be around people who love him."

"I'll allow him time with the baby, but I don't want my son to learn from his father how to treat people."

"I agree. Is mom coming over to help us?"

"Yes, Thomas is already here. He's working on the deck out back."

Once they finished painting the room, they stepped back to admire their work.

"We did good." Tiffany said.

Melanie nodded in agreement when her phone rang. She

got an uneasy feeling in her stomach when she saw it was Everett.

"Hey Melanie. I wanted to know if you'd like to go to the movies tonight?"

"Sorry, I'm busy this weekend. We are starting the remodeling of my house."

"Oh ok, can I come and help?"

"I don't think that would be a good idea. I have to go," she said and quickly ended the call.

Melanie felt like she was being too harsh on Everett. He just wanted to show he could be there for her and the baby. She was in a constant battle with herself over him.

A part of her wanted to give him a chance. She wanted to believe that he had changed and that he would be a good father. The other part of her told her she should know better. She had come a long way from the person she was before and had done a lot of healing.

Why would she ever go back to the person she had run from? She had to stop stressing about this and instead joined Tiffany to continue painting.

"Good morning, ladies," Cade said as he walked into the room.

"Hi Cade. Nice seeing you here," Tiffany said.

"Hey Tiffany, welcome back to Willow Heights." Cade said and made his way over to Melanie.

Melanie stopped painting when she noticed Cade walking over.

"What's wrong? Do I have paint on my face?" She asked when she saw a funny look on his face.

"No, not at all. You're a sight for sore eyes."

"Hilarious," she said as she looked down at her paint covered overalls.

"I'm serious. You've changed so much from when you first moved here."

"What do you mean?"

"You're much more laid back, and I don't know how to explain it. It just feels like this is where you belong. When I first met you, you always looked great but your hair was always too perfect and your clothes were all so put together."

"So now I look like a mess?"

Cade laughed and said, "No, this is coming out all wrong. You look great, Mel. You always did. But I'm really digging this look," he said as he tugged on one of her pigtails.

"Thanks. Have you eaten today?" She asked, trying to hide her blush. Tiffany was standing back, watching them with a huge smile on her face. She had clearly heard everything.

"No, I had to drive into town to grab some things and headed straight over here."

"Okay, stay here. I'll grab something for you."

Once she was in the kitchen, she overheard Tiffany and Cade talking in the living room.

"Nice seeing you back in town, Tiffany. How do you like Melanie's new house?"

"It has a lot of character, it's perfect for her and the baby."

"It's the chief's old house. He took great pride in taking care of it. Lots of memories in this old house."

"You visited them often?"

"Sure did. He has sons my age. We used to watch games and have barbecues here."

"Oh, that's nice. Why did he sell it?"

"He's retiring and moving to Texas to be closer to family. His kids moved out to Texas for college and never came back."

Melanie came back into the living room with two cups of coffee. She had made eggs, toast, and parfaits for them this morning, and they were still warm.

"Thanks Melanie."

"You're welcome, enjoy the coffee."

Melanie was seven months pregnant now and standing for long periods of time was causing her back pain. She took breaks often to rest.

While on her break, she worked on some photo frames she bought in town last week and put the sonograms in them. She also had taken photos from Mary Elle's old photo albums to hang in her hallway and throughout the house.

She noticed how much Tiffany looked like her dad and how she and Michael looked like Mary Elle.

Melanie still hadn't decided on the baby's name. She was planning on making a wooden sign with the name over the crib. Melanie was very creative and loved doing DIY projects. She had lots of things in mind and on her vision board. She had set up her vision board in the room she had decided would be the nursery. Melanie was lost in thought when Cade walked in.

"How are you feeling?"

"I'm good, just tired, my back is a little sore."

"Here, sit down and rest a bit," Cade said as he brought a seat for her and found a bucket for her to elevate her feet.

"That feels great. Thank you," Melanie said, happy to be off her feet.

"I saw your board for this room. The color you picked is very calming."

"I've read those colors help with the ambience. I want the baby to feel safe and loved."

"He's already loved by everyone. He will feel and know it without a doubt."

"You're right."

"David and some friends are here. They all agreed to help us. We need the extra help to get things done before the baby and the holidays come."

"Don't worry, I've changed my list and only need the

essential areas done. The rest can wait until after the holidays."

"We'll do as much as we can. We can quickly do most of the things on your list."

"Thanks Cade. I really appreciate all you're doing here."

"Don't worry about it. We love getting our hands dirty. Plus, this is Willow Heights. We all help each other as much as we can. Small town charm and all that," he said with a shrug.

Melanie knew she should be grateful for Cade's generosity, but she couldn't help feeling a little down by his comment. She hoped he was helping because he was interested in her, not because it was what they expected of him, because that's what they do in small towns.

Who was she kidding, anyway? Why would a guy like Cade want to get involved with a pregnant woman?

* * *

MARY ELLE ARRIVED around lunch time with pizza and chicken wings for everyone. It had been a very productive morning; the guys had almost finished installing the new countertops and painting the hallway and the nursery.

The bathroom was next. Tiffany had cleaned the chimney and Melanie was painting her new home office. Mary Elle was excited to see the progress in the house. It was already looking like Melanie had envisioned.

She spotted Melanie with Cade and she felt her heart warm. She'd known Cade for about a year now and she knew what a great guy he was. Mary Elle hadn't mentioned it to anyone, but she hoped a relationship would develop between Cade and Melanie.

"Everything's coming along so beautifully," Mary Elle said as she hugged Melanie. "I'm so proud of you. You are moving forward and standing on your own two feet," she said and then turned to face Cade before saying, "Thank you for getting everyone together and making this happen. The place is looking great!"

"It's been a pleasure," he said.

"As a special thank you, I would like to invite you to dinner at my house tomorrow night and I won't take no for an answer."

Cade laughed and said he would be there before being called away by the guy working in the bathroom.

"Thanks, Mom, for everything. The food smells delicious. Today's been a little difficult."

"Are you feeling alright?"

"Yes, I'm fine. Everett called earlier and left me feeling a little uneasy."

Melanie motioned for them to step outside so that they could speak privately. Once they were alone and out of earshot, she came clean about what else had been bothering her.

"I just don't know what to do about Everett. I don't trust him, but I want what's best for the baby and I am so torn. He gave up his rights. I should just remind him of that and move on. But, it's not that easy, is it? What if he has changed?"

"Honey, you can let him prove to you he's changed. You don't need to get back together with him. You can co-parent without being in a relationship."

"You're right. I just never thought this was what my life would be like."

"I know. No one sets out to get married and divorced. No one plans for that, but life has a funny way of always working out and I have a feeling you're going to be just fine."

"Thanks mom."

"I didn't want to say anything, but Everett came by my

house this morning. He was there pretty early. He seemed upset when I told him you weren't there."

"He called me this morning, but I was busy. He doesn't know where I bought the house. I don't know that I want him to know."

"It's up to you, but if he makes you feel uncomfortable, be honest with him and tell him."

"I've learned I have to speak up for myself. I'm not scared of him like I was before."

"Good. You shouldn't ever feel scared of your husband or boyfriend."

Tiffany found them outside and had two cups of tea with her. The afternoon turned into evening and the temperature dropped.

It was so beautiful to see the change in seasons. The leaves were turning and falling from their trees. It was almost October.

"Hey, you two left me!" Tiffany said as she joined them and handed each of them a cup of tea.

"We were just talking. How are you, sweetie?" Mary Elle asked, studying her face. She was finally worrying less about Melanie, but now her worry had turned over to Tiffany. Did moms ever get a break?

"Thanks, Tiff," Melanie said while sipping on her tea.

"Sure, thing. I'm okay, mom. Just happy to be here," she said with a sad smile.

"Have things at work gotten better?" Melanie asked.

"No, not really. I heard that they're going to cut hours and staff. I was one of the last hires, so I'm not sure what that means for my future."

Mary Elle stood back and watched her daughters. They had come such a long way, and she was proud of each one of her kiddies.

Her one wish would be to have all of them close by, but

she knew the best thing she could do was let them spread their wings and live their lives.

"I'm loving the way the kitchen is turning out. The guys are doing such a great job."

"I tried to design it to look nice and clean, but not intimidating. I want to cook with ease."

"We should go shopping tomorrow for some décor and plants."

"Sounds good."

"Girls, I have to go inside. It's too chilly for me without my sweater," Mary Elle said as she excused herself.

"Have you talked to David?"

"No, he's been busy. He looks cute with his tool belt."

"Yeah. I think we should call it a night. Everyone's worked so hard today."

"Are we driving back to mom's house to sleep there?"

"Yes, I haven't moved my bed yet. I can't sleep on an air mattress." Melanie said as she pointed to her belly and placed her hands on her hip.

* * *

As they pulled into the driveway at Mary Elle's house, they spotted an unknown vehicle parked in their driveway.

"I guess mom has visitors," Melanie said as she was getting off the car.

The girls made their way to the house, and as they walked into the living room; they saw Everett.

Tiffany hadn't seen Everett since their camping trip a few months before. She tried to keep her cool with Everett, but she was never his fan.

"Hi Everett." Tiffany said as she walked past the living room and to the kitchen, not giving Everett any chance of greeting her.

"Hi Melanie, I came by to visit and I brought this," he said as he held out a small blue teddy bear.

"Thank you."

"Mel, I invited Everett to stay for dinner. I hope that's ok." Mary Elle said as she appeared next to them.

"Sure, no problem." Melanie said as she went to put some bags away in the garage.

"How was your day?" Everett said, trying to keep his cool. He seemed annoyed at the way Melanie was treating him and she wondered if she should be nicer.

"Good, we got a lot done in the house today."

"Where's the new house?"

"Nearby."

"That's nice. You'll be close to Mary Elle."

Mary Elle had served the meal and called Melanie and Everett over to eat.

Dinner was chili, since the weather was chili outside. Mary Elle had slowly cooked it while she helped Melanie and it smelled divine.

"This is good," Everett said in-between bites.

"It truly is delicious, mom."

"I'm so happy you both are enjoying it."

Tiffany walked out of the kitchen with her bowl of chili and went to eat it on the back deck.

"Thomas said that Cade did an amazing job with the bathroom tiles," Mary Elle said.

"He really did. He's going to finish the bathroom tomorrow. We went to buy the light fixtures today."

"You hired Cade to remodel your house?" Everett asked in an annoyed tone.

"No, he offered to help me. He's a friend that offered his time."

"That's nice," Everett said, rolling his eyes

If he was trying to prove that he had changed, he was

doing a really poor job at it.

"How long are you in town for Everett?" Mary Elle asked as she served herself a glass of lemonade.

"Not long, I have to go back to work soon."

"Well, it was nice having you visit us." Mary Elle said as she walked away

"Everett, I appreciate you trying to reconnect with me and the baby, but it takes time. It will not happen overnight."

"That's why I'm here. I have a lot of paid time off to use while I figure things out with you. I want to show you I meant what I said."

"I'm trying to wrap my head around your change of heart, Everett. But I'm not sure I want to even unravel it."

* * *

SUNDAY MORNING WAS ANOTHER BLUR. They got so much done at the house. The guys worked so hard and soon it was lunchtime. They took a break and ordered Chinese food. Rita came by unexpectedly and brought some gorgeous indoor plants for Melanie to put around the house.

"These here are snake plants; they help clean the air. I got you some Peace Lily plants, ZZ plants, Begonia, and Kalanchoe which will still bloom during wintertime."

"They are beautiful, thank you Rita."

"Once everything is settled with the house and the baby, we can plan for the backyard landscaping."

"I also want some plants for the front porch."

"We can do that too."

"This house is so charming, I love it." Rita said as she looked around the house.

"Thanks Rita. I really appreciate all you do," Melanie said.

Once Rita left, and Melanie was all alone. She stood back

and admired all the work they had been put into her new home. She couldn't believe all that they had accomplished.

At the beginning of the weekend, she'd been feeling so overwhelmed, thinking she was in over her head, but Cade and Thomas had reassured her they would get it done in no time and they did.

The house was almost move-in ready. This weekend had gone by so fast. There were some minor details to take care of, which Melanie would tackle with Tiffany's help during the next couple of weekends when Tiffany had planned on coming back to visit.

She was grateful for all the hard work everyone had done to help her. It was a blessing to have such amazing friends and family. Rita's visit meant so much to Melanie. They planned to landscape in Spring. She was filled with so much gratitude for those around her. Coming from living in such a big city, she wasn't used to this.

She looked at the time and remembered she still had to get ready for dinner. Mary Elle had invited Cade to dinner tonight and Melanie wanted to attempt to look her best. Being this pregnant was tiring and sometimes she didn't have the energy to spend time on her makeup like she did back in the city.

CHAPTER 12

$\mathcal{T}$he doorbell rang, and Mary Elle knew it was Cade. Right on time, she thought as she glanced at the clock hanging on the wall. She had been trying her hardest not to butt into what was going on with Cade and Melanie, but she couldn't help herself.

She was her mother, and she only wanted what was best for Melanie. Having Everett over had reminded her of how unhappy Melanie had been for so long and how she really didn't want her to fall back into things with him. Was she being selfish for wanting what was best for her daughter? What about her grandchild? Would he be better off without Everett?

Everett said he had changed, and that he was ready to give this his all, but still actions spoke louder than words and so far, she hadn't seen anything to convince her he was this new and improved person he so desperately wanted them to believe he was.

"Good evening, Cade. How are you?" Mary Elle said as she opened the door and let Cade in.

"I'm great, Mary Elle. Thank you for having me over," he said as he handed her a gorgeous floral arrangement.

"Thank you. Thomas is running a little late, but we can have a glass of sweet tea while we wait. Melanie is almost ready for dinner."

"Sounds great."

Melanie joined them shortly after and Mary Elle couldn't help but notice the way Cade's face lit up the same way it always did when Melanie was around.

"Hi Cade," Melanie said shyly. Melanie had never been the shy type.

"Hi Melanie, you look great," Cade said and Melanie's cheeks instantly turned pink.

"Thanks."

Mary Elle saw their awkward yet sweet interaction and knew there were some undiscovered feelings there. She hoped they would realize that what they felt for each other and give it a chance to blossom.

As they were sitting in the living room conversing and have a great time, the doorbell rang.

Mary Elle got up to open the door, expecting Thomas to be there. As she opened the door, she was disappointed to find it wasn't Thomas who had rung the doorbell, it was Everett.

"Hi Everett, what a surprise to see you," Mary Elle said. She tried to disguise her disappointment.

"Hi Mary Elle, I'm here to see Melanie," Everett said as he tried to push past her.

Melanie must have overheard Everett's voice because she appeared next to Mary Elle.

"Hi Everett. I wasn't expecting to see you today."

"You look great Melanie. I came by to see if you'd like to go out to dinner with me tonight."

"I can't, Everett. I already have plans for tonight."

Everette's eyes were trained on something behind them and Mary Elle turned to see what he was staring at. It was Cade's jacket hanging on the coat rack.

"Oh, I see," Everett said.

"Maybe next time." Melanie said.

Thomas approached and greeted Everett, unknowingly inviting Everett inside. Once Thomas got inside, he knew he had a mistake in inviting Everett over for dinner. He mouthed "I'm sorry" to Melanie. Melanie nodded; she knew Thomas had meant no harm. She just wished she could get rid of Everett soon.

Everette didn't waste time and got inside to see who else was visiting Melanie. As soon as he spotted Cade, his whole body stiffened.

"Hello Cade," Everett said with a forced smile.

"Everette, isn't it?"

"Yeah, I'm Melanie's husband"

"Ex-husband," Melanie said, correcting him.

"Dinner's ready," Mary Elle announced as she ushered everyone to the dining room.

Everyone made their way to the dining room, where Mary Elle had created a very lavish feast to thank Cade for all the hard work and generosity in helping Melanie with the new house.

As they sat down, Mary Elle once again thanked Cade for everything.

"Thank you, Mary Elle, for this beautiful feast you've created. I'm honored to be of help."

Everett rolled his eyes. Mary Elle was studying Everett and knew he was the same old Everett that he had always been envious and self-serving.

They ate dinner mostly in silence, and the tension was very heavy.

"Everette, I thought you were going back home soon," Mary Elle finally said.

"I'm taking some time off work while I work things out with Melanie."

"How gracious of you," Mary Elle said.

She didn't like the way having him here was making her feel and felt it as if he was trying to force things on Melanie. This wasn't sitting right with her.

"I've assured Everett that he doesn't need to stay here in order to figure things out with me," Melanie chimed in.

"With the baby almost here, I wanted to be around in case Melanie needed help build the crib or painting the baby room," Everette said and Mary Elle used all the strength she had to not roll her eyes.

He was trying so hard to appear helpful, but it sounded too fabricated to believe.

"We completed the baby room," Cade said, catching everyone off guard.

"Yes, Cade and I finished painting and putting the baby's crib and dresser," Melanie said, smiling as she looked at Cade and he smiled back.

Mary Elle saw how Everett pushed his shoulders back and gripped on to his drink harder. His knuckles turning completely white.

"That's great," Everett said. The tension in the room was so thick you could cut it with a knife.

"Well, I guess you can always call Melanie or text her to get updates on the baby," Mary Elle said, trying to tell Everett he could leave without saying it.

"I plan on staying a little longer," Everett said, trying to keep his composure.

"One thing is for sure, this baby will completely spoiled and dotted on at all times," Thomas said as he found Mary Elle's hand on her lap and gave it a small squeeze.

Mary Elle glanced over to him and she could see in his eyes things he couldn't say out loud right now. She knew he had her back, and he was there, and he understood her concern.

She felt her shoulders instantly relax. This is what she wanted for Melanie, someone to have her back and to always be on her side. She never saw that kind of support from Everett. Not now or ever.

The rest of the dinner was silent again until Melanie excused herself. The food did not sit well with the baby and she had heartburn again.

Mary Elle got up and gave her some ginger candy that had helped Melanie with the heartburn throughout the pregnancy.

"Here you go, honey. I'm sorry about tonight."

"It's ok mom, Thomas didn't know. I don't know what to say to Everett so he can just leave me alone."

"What if you invite him into your life again? That way, you see if he's really changed or not. If he hasn't, he'll go back to his old ways and show you himself that he's just here for his own agenda, whatever that may be."

"That's a good idea. He never enjoyed doing things with me and I'm sure he'll hate going to the doctor appointment and buying groceries or going shopping for the baby."

"Just try it and remember when you're not ok with him being around too close or often you may speak up and let him know. He really has no parental rights over the baby."

"I know, mom. I understand."

* * *

BOTH CADE and Everett sat around, not sure what to do. They were both on guard and neither was willing to go first. Finally, Everett received a call on his phone and left. Melanie was glad to see him go. She always felt better when he wasn't around.

"I should probably get going, too. It's late," Cade said.

"Thank you for coming. Sorry about tonight."

"It's ok. I understand that you're in a complicated situation right now. I really enjoy your company a lot and that's probably why I should go."

"What do you mean?"

"You and Everett have things to work out, and I don't want to get in the way of that. You need to decide what you think is best for your child."

"Thank you for being so understanding."

A part of her wanted to ask him to stay. She wanted to spend more time with him. She wanted to know everything there was to know about him, but she knew he was right.

Melanie needed to figure things out with Everett first.

They said their goodbyes and as soon as he was gone; she texted Everett.

"Since you want to be a part of the process with me and the baby, you're welcome to come to my doctor's appointment tomorrow afternoon."

"Sure, thing. I'll pick you up at work."

"Ok, we have to be there by 2pm."

"I get it," he replied.

Melanie thought she was seeing his old pattern coming through, which in a way meant she had been right about him all this time.

CHAPTER 13

*T*he next day, Everett showed up at Willow Acres and texted Melanie he was outside waiting for her. She thought he would've gotten out to help her, but no, he didn't.

Since she was leaving home for the day, she had to bring her laptop, her lunchbox, purse and a small bag with extra clothing in. Her belly had gotten bigger as she's now in her eighth month of pregnancy.

As she approached the car, she saw Everett's annoyed face. It took her back when they were married and every little thing she did would upset him.

"Hey can you open your trunk so I can put my bags in there?" Melanie asked, not surprised he hadn't gotten out to help her with everything she was carrying.

Chivalry wasn't there with Everett. As he pushed the button to open the trunk, David appeared and rushed to help Melanie put everything in the trunk.

"Here, let me help you Melanie," David said as he took the things from her and put them in the trunk.

"Thanks David."

"No problem, I'll see you tomorrow."

"Bright and early. We have a meeting early in the morning with a new client." Melanie reminded David.

"Yes, I almost forgot. We'll talk later."

As Melanie got in the car she was greeted by Everett's annoyed sigh.

"Let's go. Here's the address in case you want to put it in the GPS," Melanie said, and she felt that sinking feeling in her stomach that she always felt around Everett. She hadn't missed that at all.

"You can guide me,"

"Ok, well it's in the next town."

"You couldn't get a doctor here?"

"No."

Everett sighed and asked, "How was your day?"

"Great, how was yours?" Melanie asked.

"Fine. I hope we aren't late for the appointment."

Little did Everett know that time in the countryside was slower and things were relaxed compared to hustle and bustle of the city. She knew that even if they were on time for the appointment, it would be a little while before the doctor saw her and that she would actually take her time to ask her how she was feeling and go over what to expect next; especially now that she was close to being eight months pregnant with her first child.

Melanie walked into the doctor's office and checked in with Beth, the receptionist. She was a cute college girl that was always friendly. Everett sat down, already bored, and quickly got on his cellphone to check emails from work.

As always, there was no attempt on his part to have any communication with Melanie or any type of interaction. Another couple walked in and checked in with Beth, and they sat down across from Melanie and Everett.

The couple smiled at each other and were visibly happy

to be together. They had a baby name book and were picking out names for their baby. Melanie longed to have that, but she knew Everett would never be capable of giving her those moments or that kind of attention. Everett was too engrossed on his phone to even notice how he was acting, just like he did back in the day. Melanie took a deep breath and allowed Everett to prove her wrong... or right.

A few minutes passed, and Everett went up to Beth and asked how much longer it would be before they called Melanie in.

"It'll be a few more minutes, sir," Beth said.

"Thanks," Everett replied with a dissatisfied look.

As he was walking back to sit with Melanie, his phone rang. He said he would be back soon and stepped outside to take the call.

Melanie peeked outside and saw him standing on the sidewalk, looking away from the doctor's office. She opened the office door and tried to hear what he was saying. All she got was, "I'm at the doctor's office with her now. I'm trying my best to convince her. It's harder than we thought."

Then Beth called her name, and she closed the doctor's office.

Who could be calling Everett and talking about his efforts to win her back? Why was he complaining that it was harder than they thought? She had more suspicions about his efforts to restore their marriage, but who would care enough to call and ask him about it?

Melanie couldn't focus on that now. She had to see Dr. Banks. Melanie asked Beth if she could get Everett for her since she didn't want him to know she had eavesdropped on him. Dr. Banks had already started checking on Melanie when Everett stepped into the exam room.

"Dr. Banks, this is my ex-husband, Everett. He is visiting and wanted to accompany me on the appointment today."

"Nice to meet you, Everett. I'm Dr. Banks. I will help Melanie deliver the baby."

"Nice to meet you as well."

"Melanie, how have you been? Anything new?"

"I've gained back the weight I had lost. My heartburn has gotten better with the ginger candy. The weight of the belly is causing a lot of back pain for me. He's been moving a lot in there with very little space."

"He?" Everett said with a slight smile.

"Yes, it's a baby boy," Dr. Banks answered. "that's great Melanie. He's a big boy. He's currently 7lbs. That's big for your petite frame. Let's do an ultrasound to make sure he's ok in there."

Dr. Banks poured the jelly over Melanie's belly and got the ultrasound going. The baby's heartbeat was strong, and he was bouncing around in there.

"He looks great. He's almost ready to come out and join us."

"I'm so excited! I can't wait to meet him," Melanie said, smiling with tears of joy. She was so much more emotional now because of the pregnancy.

Everett was speechless. It seemed as if hearing the baby's heartbeat made it all too real for him. Everett had shared many times with Melanie his uneasy feelings about becoming a father.

It was as if he wanted to experience it, but was afraid he would not be a good father because he wouldn't have time to spend with any children and because that had been his experience growing up. His father owned several companies in different states and was rarely home.

His dad made up for his absence with gifts and trips, but he was never really involved in Everett's life. Being successful was much more important and interesting than spending time with the family.

Susan, Everett's mother, had several nannies to take care of Everett when she went off on her trips with her friends. They almost sent him to boarding school in the UK to make sure he was worldly, but luckily, Everett's mother opposed since he was an only child and she wasn't ready to send him off overseas.

After the doctor's appointment, Everett was extremely quiet. Melanie didn't want to upset him again and remained silent for the drive to Mary Elle's house.

"Here we are," Melanie said as she was getting out of the car, "could you pop the trunk open?"

"Yeah," Everett replied with a puzzled look on his face, as if he's still processing the baby's heartbeat.

"Look, I understand it's a lot for you. You didn't really want this and now we are in this situation. Just know I'm completely fine with you not being involved and I'm sorry I didn't tell you it's a baby boy."

"I just need time to figure things out for me," Everett said as he reached down to push the trunk button.

* * *

As Melanie walked into Mary Elle's house, DeeAnn greeted her.

"Hey Sweetheart, here let me help you."

"Thanks Aunt D, it's getting difficult to walk and carry things. The baby is getting bigger and soon will position himself to come out."

"Oh, you had a doctor's appointment today?"

"Yes, and Everett came along."

"How was that?"

"He was impatient in the waiting room and after hearing the baby's heartbeat, he was silent and then just absent-minded. He said he needed time to think about things for himself. I don't know what he meant by that."

"Well, he's always been strange from what I've gathered," DeeAnn said with a small laugh.

"I'm starving, I'll make dinner."

"No, don't worry. I made dinner already. Freshen up and I'll have it served for you."

"Thanks Auntie, I'll be back."

DeeAnn had bought some pho from the new restaurant in town. Their grand opening was over the weekend and it had already a lot of great reviews. DeeAnn and Melanie ate the pho and caught up since it had been a long time since DeeAnn was home for dinner.

CHAPTER 14

*M*ary Elle was so excited for today that she hadn't slept all week. It had been extremely difficult to keep the secret from Melanie and hide all her plans.

She thought she was getting better at scheming. Maybe she should be a spy or detective instead of an event planner, she thought as she giggled to herself.

"Mom, are you okay?" Tiffany asked, eyeing her suspiciously.

"Oh, I'm fine. Is everyone on the way? Where is your sister? Does she know?"

"Relax, mom. Melanie does not know that you have planned the most top-secret baby shower ever."

"Oh, I hope you're right."

"Hey Fam!" Ruby said as she walked in, followed close behind by Brittney and Michael.

"My baby!" Mary Elle said as she pulled Michael into a big hug.

"Wow, I see who the favorite is." Tiffany said as she hugged her brother.

"Thank you for getting these guys from the airport, Ruby."

"It was my pleasure. It's always great catching up with Brittney, Michael, not so much." Ruby said with a laugh, and Michael rolled his eyes.

Mary Elle smiled at their banter. Just like old times, she thought.

"How can we help?" Brittney asked, always ready to jump into action.

"The guys are outback setting up the tables. You girls could help take the floral arrangements out back," Mary Elle said as she guided them to the dining table where the floral arraignments Patty had prepared the night before were waiting.

The girls gathered the floral arraignments and made their way to the backyard, leaving Michael and Mary Elle alone.

"How have you been, sweetie?" Mary Elle asked, studying Michael. He lived out in California and she hadn't seen him in almost a year.

"I'm great, mom. There's actually something I wanted to tell you."

"What is it?"

"I'm engaged."

Mary Elle let out a small gasp and broke into a big smile, "Engaged? With who? I didn't even know you had a girlfriend!"

"Her name is Samantha. We've been dating for about six months now."

"Is she here? When are we meeting her?"

"She couldn't make it today, but she will be here for Christmas."

"Oh, Michael! I am so happy for you," Mary Elle said as she pulled him in for another hug.

Michael had never had a serious girlfriend and Mary Elle

had often worried that he would never get married. She couldn't wait to meet her future daughter-in-law.

She must be a very special girl to get her eldest child to settle down.

Mary Elle was caught completely off guard when she saw who came through the door next.

"Susan! What are you doing here?"

"Everett told me the baby shower was today and I wouldn't miss it for the world."

Mary Elle had debated letting Everett know about the baby shower, but since Melanie let him be a part of the baby's life, she figured she would let him know. She didn't want any bad blood between them.

"There's still a couple of hours before the shower starts," Mary Elle said.

"I came early in case there was anything I could help with."

That caught Mary Elle by surprise. Maybe Everett and his mom had changed? She knew kids often brought many together. Maybe this baby would unite them?

"Okay, great! Let's head outside and see what we can do?"

* * *

IT WAS ALMOST time for Melanie to come by Willow Acres. Mary Elle had asked her to come by the office because she needed help to print some brochures.

Little did Melanie know it was her baby shower. Melanie hadn't made a big deal about having a baby shower, but Mary Elle couldn't help herself and started planning for the baby shower months in advance. Mary Elle had been so careful with every detail to make sure it would be a complete surprise for Melanie.

She had arranged with Thomas to use the back parking

lot so there weren't any cars that Melanie would recognize and have any suspicions.

Melanie walked into her mother's office where Mary Elle and Thomas were waiting for her. They printed a copy of the brochure and then Mary Elle asked Melanie if they could go for a walk by the lake.

As soon as they got to the lake, Melanie spotted her friends and family and she saw big blue balloons and the tables and chairs that were arranged.

As they got closer, the crowd yelled "Surprise!"

She said her hello's to everyone and quickly scanned the room, and she saw Michael, Ruby, Cade, Tiffany, David, Thomas, and the rest of the gang.

Melanie's heart was full of love and gratitude. She really wasn't expecting a baby shower. The floral arraignments and all the decorations were amazing. Mary Elle had really put all her effort and love into this baby shower.

They had set up a lovely table with a big comfy chair adorned with blue and white balloons for Melanie to sit and enjoy the food and drinks that Mary Elle had ordered for her special girl.

As she sat down, Everett and Susan made their way to greet her. Melanie had not noticed them until now.

"Hello Melanie," Susan said through gritted teeth. It was as if being there and seeing all the love that everyone had for Melanie and her baby were eating her up with envy.

Melanie noticed and felt bad for Susan.

"Hi Susan, nice to see you again."

Looking around Susan said, "Lovely to be here."

"Hi Everett," Melanie said, turning her attention to Everett who looked uncomfortable and like he was being forced to put on a smiling face.

She couldn't believe she had once called him her husband,

it seemed like so long ago. Had things between them always been this awkward and cold?

"Hi Melanie, what an elaborate party Mary Elle has really outdone herself."

"Yes, it's beautiful. Glad you could make it. I hope you both have a great time here."

"I won't stay for long; I have other places to be," Susan said.

"Well, it's great having you here," Melanie said as she went on her way to the photo booth Mary Elle had set up with different props, where she spotted Tiffany and Michael.

"Michael, it's so great to see you again!" Melanie said as she hugged him and then she noticed Ruby and Brittney standing nearby and called them over.

"Ruby, it's been forever!" Melanie said as she hugged her, but the baby bump prevented the embrace.

"You are glowing, Mel. You look amazing" Ruby said, and they took several photos with little handheld signs that read "Baby on the way", "It's a boy!", "Mommy to be", among others and Melanie's favorite "Get Him Out!"

The balloon arch was beautiful. It had baby blue and golden balloons that varied in sizes and at right side of the arch there was a Mama Bear with a baby bear and gorgeous autumn flowers.

The dessert and food table were full of exquisite treats like: individual Shepard's pies, ham & cheese biscuit stacks, pretzel bread bowl with cheese dip, pulled pork doughnut hole sliders, ham and brie pastries, deviled eggs, caprese salad kabobs, lemon-lime punch, blueberry lemon trifle, fruit kabobs with cream cheese dip, cotton candy champagne cocktails, charcuterie board, among other yummy things.

* * *

MELANIE WAS ENJOYING her baby shower; the food and drinks were amazing. They also had the traditional baby shower games like bobbing for pacifiers, don't say baby, don't drop the egg baby, diaper change relay race, among other games.

Surprisingly, David was an expert diaper changer and Thomas managed to keep the egg from dropping the longest. It was so much fun to see everyone relaxed and laughing and having a great time. There was no work talk or anyone that didn't belong there. Melanie felt so much love from everyone, and she knew the baby would feel it as well.

Mary Elle and David hired a photographer to take endless photos of all the activities and guests and to capture those spontaneous moments that always seemed to make the best memories. Cade tried his best to always be at Melanie's side, showing her support, and was the perfect gentleman. Everyone was having a great time and enjoying themselves.

Susan and Everett were still standing in a corner like outcasts. They had refused to partake in any games and hadn't touched the food. Melanie didn't know why they even bothered coming.

"We got to get going," David said as he appeared next to Cade." We need to head out to Chad's cabin to fish. Remember?"

"Yeah, I have my stuff in my car," Cade said as he turned to Melanie and said, "I hope you enjoyed your baby shower. Thanks for inviting me," and pulled her into a hug.

"Thank you both for coming. Have a great fishing trip." Melanie said, trying to keep her cool and not show all the emotions that were swirling inside her.

Melanie made her way over to the restroom after Cade and David left. On her way there, she overheard Susan saying very firmly, "Everett, you have to work harder to get Melanie to get back with you. I'm running out of patience; the baby will be born soon and I want to be a grandmother. Don't forget our deal. You'll be in charge of the baby's trust fund if you make this happen. You're my only child, and this might be the only chance I get to be a grandmother. Your funds are almost gone Everett, if you want to keep up with a life of luxury and only work because it's your passion. You have to get back with Melanie and be a father."

Everett groaned like a child having a tantrum and said, "Mom, I'm trying. I just don't want to be a father. When the baby's ultrasound was being done, I felt nothing. I think there's something wrong with me. I tried, but I don't feel a connection to the child or Melanie. Maybe I'm not supposed to be a father."

"Don't say that, just win Melanie back and she'll take care of the baby."

"I'll try, but I can't promise. I'm your son and I've misused my money with this gambling addiction, but you have to help me."

Melanie couldn't believe what she had just heard. Everett was only using the baby to get money from his mother? She couldn't believe she had let him talk her into letting him back into her life. She looked towards her family and they were all taking silly photos at the photo boot again. Melanie didn't want to interrupt them. She only wanted to be alone.

CHAPTER 15

*M*elanie had snuck away from the party and was headed towards her house. She didn't know what to feel or think. She knew Everett hadn't really changed, but how dare he use her baby?

By the time she reached her house, it was raining, and she didn't have an umbrella, but she made a run for it.

She walked into her house and rested her back against the door once she was inside. It took her a minute to catch her breath and to clear her mind.

She'd been feeling some pain all day, but she figured it was too early to be having contractions. Melanie hadn't mentioned anything because she wasn't sure if she was over-reacting. Now that she was alone in her house and the pain was becoming more persistent, she was getting nervous.

She grabbed her phone to call her mother, but of course she didn't have service. Service in Willow Heights was always spotty. That was the only thing she missed about the city.

She jumped at the sound of banging coming from the nursery.

"Hello? Is anyone there?" she asked, but no one answered and the banging went on.

"Come out now!" she said and looked around for something to defend herself with. She grabbed a cast iron shovel from her fireplace tool kit.

"This will have to do," she said to herself. She sent a mental thank you over to Tiffany for making her take self-defense lessons when she moved to New York, and she hoped they would come in handy today.

She headed towards the room where all the noise was coming from. She tried to turn on the light but she remembered that they never got around to adding a light bulb to this room.

"I have a weapon and I am not afraid to use it!" she called out as she went into the room, but the noises didn't stop. Was this thief deaf? What was going on?

A bright light suddenly blinded her, and she let out a yelp, dropping the shovel. So much for self-defense.

"Melanie?"

"Cade? What are you doing here? Why aren't you fishing?"

"David hadn't packed yet, and I wanted to surprise you by finishing the baby's closet before you got home. Didn't you see my car out-front?"

"No, I was a little preoccupied," she said before she let out a small cry and hunched over in pain.

"Are you okay? What's wrong?" Cade said, coming closer and resting a hand on her back.

"I don't know. I've been having these pains all day. They come and go but they are getting worse."

"Are they contractions?"

"I don't know. I'm not due yet."

"Let's get you to the hospital."

"My hospital bag is in my car and I don't have any cell service."

"Okay, I'll grab it and I'll call your mom once we have service."

Melanie couldn't help but feel grateful to have Cade in her life. She couldn't even imagine what would have happened if he wasn't there to help her get to the hospital. She hoped and prayed that she wasn't in labor, since she still had a couple of weeks left before her due date.

As they got closer to Main Street, the cellphone reception was better.

"Mom, don't panic, but I'm going to the hospital. Cade is driving me," Melanie said, holding in the pain of another contraction.

"Ok, sweetie. I'll be there soon," Mary Elle said as she quickly ended the call.

"How are you feeling, Mel?" Cade asked as he helped Melanie out of the car and into a wheelchair.

"I'm ok for now. I texted Dr. Banks. She'll be here soon," Melanie said.

* * *

THEY ADMITTED MELANIE, and she had her own private room. Mary Elle and the rest of the gang joined Melanie in her room.

Cade was holding her hand as each contraction came.

"How are you feeling, Melanie?" Michael asked as he handed her a cup of water.

"I'm ok, just having some pain."

"Are you ready to meet your baby?" Ruby asked as she appeared from behind Michael.

"I guess I am."

Tiffany appeared beside them and asked, "So, what's the baby's name?"

"I have a few names in mind, but my favorite is Ryder. His complete name will be Ryder Cole Blackburn."

"He'll have our last name? I love it!" Tiffany said.

Melanie had hidden her name choice from them all because she didn't want to have to explain herself and with Everett around, she didn't want him partaking in choosing the baby's name or having to argue about the baby's last name.

"Yes, he is my son. He will have my last name."

"What a noble name for a boy," Michael said.

"Michael, I'm so happy you're here. We never get to see you, but having you here for this special moment in my life is exactly as it should be."

"There's something I want to share with you all now that we are here together," Michael said as he looked at the group of friends and family. "I'm engaged."

"What?" Tiffany said in shock.

"I met a girl while I was traveling for work and we've been dating for six months now and recently got engaged."

"Wow, I did not see that coming. Who is she?" Melanie asked while looking at Ruby, who was clearly shocked and sad after hearing the news.

Melanie knew Ruby had been in love with Michael for a long time now, but she never told him because he never saw Ruby as more than a sister since they had grown up together.

"She's a flight attendant, and she'll be joining us for Christmas," Michael answered.

Dr. Banks appeared to check on Melanie and the room cleared, leaving only Mary Elle with Melanie.

"Let's see Melanie, I'll check to see how dilated you are," Dr. Banks said as she was putting on her sterile gloves.

Mary Elle stood next to Melanie's bed and held her hand.

"Everything looks wonderful. The baby is positioned and looks like they are real contractions and your cervix is about 6 cm dilated."

"Oh, my goodness, Melanie, you're in labor," Mary Elle said as her eyes filled with tears of joy, "Let me go tell them in the waiting room."

Dr. Banks explained that she didn't need to push just yet and they will continue to monitor her and the baby. Melanie opted to hold off on the epidural for now. She was still withstanding the pain and was doing her breath-work. Dr. Banks recommended Melanie try to rest now before the contractions got stronger and faster, but said she could have visitors.

Everyone came back into the room to take part in Melanie's special day. They filled the room with so much love, there was no way the baby wouldn't know how much they loved him. Cade made his way next to Melanie's bed and told her some jokes to keep her mind from any worries. He was an amazing friend and Melanie wished that friendship would soon turn into something more. She knew her feelings for him were real and strong. She wasn't afraid of falling for him. He was a great guy that had always shown his heart and intentions toward her.

* * *

AFTER ABOUT 8 HOURS, Melanie was ready to push. Mary Elle was by her side, holding her hand and Tiffany was on her other side, encouraging her to push and be strong. Melanie opted to not have an epidural and feel everything. She wanted this experience to be natural. Soon, baby Ryder was born. Both Mary Elle and Tiffany helped cut the cord. He gave out a nice, robust cry. They quickly cleaned him up, weighed and measured. Ryder weighed 7 lbs and 3 oz. They wrapped him up in a blanket and handed him to Melanie.

"Hi beautiful boy," Melanie said, kissing his forehead.

Melanie was tired from pushing and staying up all night, but holding Ryder gave her energy and she felt a warm feeling inside her. She knew it was a special kind of love she was feeling for the first time. Melanie stared at Ryder and was amazed at what God had gifted her with. She knew her life would never be the same. She was now a mother. Melanie thanked God for helping her through all the difficult times she had during her pregnancy and for giving her the strength to push through it all to be here with Ryder now.

* * *

MARY ELLE STAYED in the room with Melanie and took several photos with her cellphone. Tiffany stepped outside to let everyone know the baby was born and told them they could come inside to meet Ryder.

"Hi Melanie," Thomas said quietly as he walked into the room with flowers and balloons.

"Hi Thomas," Melanie said before she noticed Michael, Ruby, Cade and David walking in after Thomas.

Everyone was here to welcome Ryder. There was so much love in the room, it was perfect. Melanie felt so blessed to have such great friends and family.

Melanie handed the baby to Mary Elle, who started crying tears of joy as soon as she held him. "He looks like you Melanie," Mary Elle said.

"Can I hold him?" Tiffany asked, eager to meet her first nephew.

"Sure," Mary Elle said as she handed Ryder to Tiffany.

Mary Elle and Michael were taking lots of photos with their cellphones.

Soon everyone took a turn holding Ryder. After a while, baby Ryder cried. He was hungry.

Mary Elle asked for privacy and everyone cleared the room and went to have lunch in the hospital's cafeteria.

Melanie breastfed Ryder. Mary Elle was there to help her when he didn't latch on right. After a big meal, Ryder fell asleep. Mary Elle helped Melanie burp Ryder as she slept. The nurse came to take the baby to the nursery to allow Mary Elle and Melanie to rest.

"Did you call Everett?" Melanie asked.

"No, I haven't. Do you want me to?"

"No. I want to enjoy these precious moments."

"Ok, no worries. I called your dad and he'll be here tomorrow. He's on a business trip in England. He said he was going to catch a flight as soon as he could to be here tomorrow at the latest."

"It's ok, tell him to take his time."

"I sent him several photos of you and the baby. I called Rita; she'll be here in a few hours."

"Thanks mom."

Melanie had so much to be grateful for. God had answered all her prayers. She was a mom now, and Ryder was healthy and beautiful. She was also thankful for the bad times she had experienced, because those had taught her to not take anything or anyone for granted. They had also guided her to Willow Heights and to her new home. She had found her home and wouldn't trade the magic of Willow Heights for any big city life.

EPILOGUE

*M*elanie woke up on Thanksgiving morning surprised to see that she had slept a full eight hours. It had been two weeks since Ryder was born and she hadn't slept for longer than three hours at a time.

Everette found out about the baby's birth via social media. It didn't bother him one bit to have missed it. Susan had been furious. She called Melanie, demanding to see the baby. Melanie reminded her that Everette terminated all his parental rights and Ryder was her son and she would think about allowing her to meet him down the road someday.

Susan wasn't very pleased but understood as her lawyers had read and reviewed all the divorce papers and confirmed what Melanie was saying was true. She had no basis for making any demands or threats about spending time with the baby.

Melanie made her way to the kitchen and found her mother making breakfast. Mary Elle had insisted on spending the night to give Melanie a much needed break.

"Good morning, sweetheart. How are you feeling?"

"I'm feeling great, mom. Where's Ryder?"

"He's in his nursery," Mary Elle said as she continued on making breakfast.

Melanie heard Ryders nursery tunes playing as she got closed and she could hear someone singing. She figured it was Thomas, but as she walked into the room, she found Cade. He was holding Ryder, and she felt her heart flip-flop in her chest.

"Happy thanksgiving," he said when he spotted her.

"Good morning. Happy thanksgiving to you too. What are you doing here?"

"You said your sink was leaking, so I came over to fix it. I couldn't leave without seeing the little guy first."

"Thanks Cade. You're so great. I didn't expect you to come fix it. I'm sorry that I'm always giving you extra work."

"You don't give me extra work and I enjoy helping you," Cade said as he placed Ryder back in his crib.

"I know, but" she began to say.

"Stop."

"Stop what?"

"Stop talking, please" Cade said as he made his way over to Melanie and stood right in front of her.

"Okay," she said as she noticed their proximity. Her heart started beating faster. She began to fiddle with her bracelet.

"How do you feel about dinner?" Cade asked, as he took her hands in his.

"Dinner is good. I love having dinner."

Cade laughed, "How do you feel about having dinner with me tomorrow night?"

"Like a date?" Melanie asked, to be sure.

"Yes," Cade said, his smile widening.

"I'd love that," Melanie said as she broke into a smile.

* * *

THIS YEAR'S Thanksgiving dinner was being held at Mary Elle's house. She had spent all day cooking and getting everything ready after she'd gotten back from Melanie's house. Bill and Barb were attending along with Rita and Bob.

"Look at this beautiful boy," Bill said as he walked into Mary Elle's house and took the baby from Melanie. Barbara trailed close behind him.

"Hi Dad, Hi Barb. Welcome," Melanie said.

"Melanie, it's nice to see you," Barb said as she entered the home.

"Bill, Barb, please come and sit with us," Mary Elle said gesturing them to come sit in the living room with Thomas, David, and Cade.

"Thanks for having us, Mary Elle," Bill said.

Mary Elle introduced everyone and was happy to see them getting along and making small talk.

"Dad!" Tiffany said as she walked into the living room with a drink tray.

"Sweetie, how are you?"

"I'm great. Hi Barb. Nice to see you." Tiffany said politely.

Shortly after, Rita and Bob arrived and joined them in the living room for drinks and hors d'oeuvres.

As usual, Mary Elle had outdone herself with decorations and meal planning. Everything was elegant, with a hint farmhouse style. It was so great to see everyone happy and not arguing.

Mary Elle had moved on and had forgiven Bill and Barb. She was living her life to the fullest. She was now a grandmother, something that made her extremely proud. Bill seemed happy with Barb and Barb seemed like, well, Barb.

Tiffany mentioned she was happy to see her parents in the same room again and being cordial with each other. Rita and Bob also seemed happy to see everyone together again.

The dinner was splendid, everything was delicious.

Thomas made a toast. It was beautiful and as he concluded, he said: "I'm a very blessed man. I couldn't ask God for anything else in life. He's given everything I've ever dreamt of, including the most beautiful and gracious, Mary Elle," Thomas said as he stood closer to Mary Elle and took her hand before going down on one knee, "Mary Elle, will you be my wife?"

The shock in Mary Elle's face was real, and it was clear she wasn't expecting to be proposed to today, but with no hesitation she said, "Yes!"

Without a doubt, this year was full of trials and tribulations, but what mattered most was that everyone was there together. They all had so many blessings to be grateful for and so much had changed, but it had all turned out the way it was meant to.

THANK you for reading Finally Home in Willow Heights. I hope you enjoyed it! The next book in the series is Christmas in Willow Heights. Click here if you'd like to join Mary Elle and the rest of the gang on the next book. The fourth book in the series, The Inn at Willow Heights can be found here.

LET'S BE FRIENDS!

JOIN ABIGAIL'S Newsletter for reminders of upcoming releases.

JOIN ABIGAIL'S Reader Group for: First Looks, exclusive giveaways, and more!

Made in the USA
Monee, IL
25 March 2022